Connections

CW00539872

ADA

Katharine E. Smith

HEDDON PUBLISHING

First edition published in 2024 by Heddon Publishing.

ISBN 978-1-913166-98-4
Ebook 978-1-913166-99-1

Cover design by Catherine Clarke Design
www.catherineclarkedesign.co.uk

www.heddonpublishing.com
www.facebook.com/heddonpublishing
@PublishHeddon

Katharine E. Smith is the author of nineteen novels, including the bestselling Coming Back to Cornwall series. *Ada* is the fourth book of the Connections series – also set in Cornwall, but quite different. Katharine's newest series is What Comes Next and is set – for a change – in Shropshire, where she lives with her husband, their two children, and two excitable dogs.

A Philosophy graduate, Katharine initially worked in the IT and charity sectors. She turned to freelance editing in 2009, which led to her setting up Heddon Publishing, working with independent authors across the globe.

You can find details of her books on her website:
www.katharineesmith.com

Information about her work with other authors can be found here:
www.heddonpublishing.com
and here:
www.heddonbooks.com

For Jenny, Neil, Sam & Polly

ADA

A brief who's who, in the Connections books so far:

Elise (Connections Book One). Ninety-something, mother of Louisa and Laurie, grandmother of Ada.

Louisa (Connections Book Three). Daughter of Elise, mother of Ada.

Jude. Louisa's partner. Runs the local foodbank.

Ada (Connections Book Four). The subject of this book! Daughter of Louisa, granddaughter of Elise.

Laurie. Son of Elise, brother of Louisa, uncle of Ada. Lives on a remote Scottish Isle as a wildlife warden.

AJ. Louisa's ex-colleague & ex-lover, but there's even more to him than this. In case you haven't read book three (Louisa) let's just say it's complicated.

Maggie (Connections Book Two). Mother of Stevie, daughter of Lucy, twin sister of Julia, friend of Elise.

Stevie. Teenage daughter of Maggie.

Lucy. Mother of Maggie, grandmother of Stevie.

Tony. Maggie's partner and Louisa's ex-colleague.

Julia. Maggie's twin sister.

Ada

I can't believe that I've finished university. Already! I honestly feel like my feet have barely touched the floor, and now I have to leave. Some of my friends are staying on here but I know already that it's not for me. The question is, where next? Now Mum's left London and the only home I've ever known, I don't have a base there, and my lifelong friend Clara is staying up in Birmingham so she won't be around either. Everything has changed and it's all been out of my hands.

"How are you feeling?" Mum asked me when she came to collect my things. We'd gone out for lunch, at a restaurant overlooking the pebble beach.

"Great!" I'd replied cheerily, but in honesty I just feel flat.

The last few days have seen an exodus of students from this part of town, and the surrounding streets have become eerily quiet. There are families and older residents still scattered along these terraces, and I'm sure for them it's a relief, but for me it feels a little bit lonely. I could have left too, with Mum, which would have saved me rattling around this nearly empty house, but it's a long way to go to Cornwall and then come nearly all the way back again for the weekend at Josh's.

I do at least have that to look forward to. *One last hoorah*, as he said ironically.

There are nine of us going to his parents' place, and in my imagination it's going to be like one of those country weekends you read about in old novels, with riding and hunting and shooting; even though the majority of us who are going are vegetarian, and Josh himself is vegan – apparently much to his parents' disappointment.

"Dad's a true country sports type," he's said disparagingly. Josh has told me that he was taken fox-hunting as a child, and he hated it.

"I thought fox hunting was illegal," drawled Sasha. She knows full well it is; her parents come from the same 'set' as Josh's, or his dad at least.

Josh's mum is 'new money', having married into the small but strange world that they inhabit – and even still holding down a job when financially she has no need to.

Josh looked at the joint Sasha was passing across to him, and the stream of smoke escaping her mouth and nostrils. "So is smoking weed."

"Fair point!" She had laughed and coughed. "But at least it's not hurting anybody."

"That's not necessarily true," I'd said. "Who knows where this stuff is coming from? What if it's some kind of county lines operation?"

"Alright, alright," Sasha had laughed again. "Anyone would think you two were hunt supporters though!"

"Absolutely not," I had said firmly. "But we've got to take responsibility for what we're doing too."

"Ada's right," said Archie, which had made my heart skip a beat.

I try not to think about Archie too much because it's just so obvious, fancying him. All the girls do – some of the boys, too. It's not only about his looks but his general air of confidence and attitude to life. And for me, though I try not to think of this too much, there's also his similarity to somebody from my not-too-distant past.

I suspect that once we've left here Archie won't look back, to these lazy, hazy student days, but I know I'm going to miss them so much. The shared houses, the rooms full of friends, impromptu parties, late night discussions, PlayStation marathons. It's not real life, I know (and I will say I really have worked hard as well), but it's been so much fun. And I've felt like I've been part of something new and exciting; a burning ball of energy with the potential to create something amazing. To initiate change and make the world a better place. We share the same ideals, many of my friends and me, and that is such a good feeling. We feed off each other and energise each other, back each other up.

Now, we're disbanding. Disappearing back in all directions, to family homes. Becoming daughters and sons again; sisters and brothers; returning to childhood bedrooms and single beds. Looking for jobs. Learning about the 'real world'. The fireball is fizzling out.

2006

When Ada started school, her mum had been worried that she might feel different to the other children. A girl without a dad. With a mum much older than anyone else's. But in actual fact, lots of Ada's friends came from a variety of backgrounds, and these things never crossed her mind until she was much older; even then, only briefly. Instead, on that hot September day, four-year-old Ada was just excited. While Louisa had been worrying, her daughter had been looking forward to being a grown-up schoolgirl. Having her own school bag, and lunchbox, and PE kit.

Even so, as the two of them approached the gates, the anticipation transformed into a fluttering of nervousness in her tummy, which her mum said were butterflies.

"Really? In my tummy?" Ada wasn't sure she liked that idea.

"Not literally," Louisa said, in her grown-up way and Ada felt proud that she knew what 'literally' meant. "It's a saying. Because feeling nervous can make you feel a bit unsettled in your stomach, like there are butterflies in there."

Years later, Ada will still remember this exact conversation, which took place just before they entered the playground. She will remember too hanging onto her mum's legs as Louisa gently tried to extricate her daughter and hand her over to one of the teaching assistants.

Louisa was trying not to think about work but she knew she had to get her daughter into school and then dash to the tube station if she was going to make it to her meeting. She had been determined, though, that it would be she who dropped Ada off on her momentous first day.

Parents and childminders and small children converged at the double door that led into the reception classroom, forming a slight crowd. Some already knew each other and were laughing and chatting as though this was the most natural thing in the world. Those with older children were acting nonchalant, being old hands at all this. Louisa felt her grip tighten on her daughter's hand and something like panic in the pit of her stomach, at the thought of just letting Ada go in there, with all these unknown people.

It's just school, she told herself, surreptitiously taking a long, slow inhale and then smiling brightly at Ada. *Just school.*

She looked around her, feeling very old in comparison to many of the other mums, and trying to catch the eye of a responsible adult so that she could hand Ada over and know she was safe. There! She recognised a teaching assistant from the taster day Ada had come to and, summoning her steely work persona, edged determinedly forwards with Ada by her side.

"Miss Watson! Good morning. Here's Ada." Louisa gently pulled her daughter's hands from her legs, trying to push away the feeling of guilt that was nagging at her for being so keen to offload her little girl.

It wasn't like that really, but she assumed it would seem that way to the teaching assistant.

"You have a good day Ada, and be good, OK?" Louisa said, and she dared a quick hug before pulling back and checking that Ada was alright. She wasn't wailing. She didn't look pale or distressed. And this in itself made Louisa's insides squeeze together like an accordion. She had never realised how hard she could love, until her daughter had come along.

"Hello Ada," Miss Watson had said, smiling at Louisa before turning fully to the little girl. "Shall we go and find you a peg for your bag? And then you can go in and play with the other children. We've got lots of toys out, do you want to see?"

And that was that. Miss Watson took control, exactly as Louisa had wanted her to. This was how it worked. Louisa Morgan was used to making things happen.

While her mum half-walked, half-jogged away, trying to swallow back her tears, Ada Morgan walked into the school with the teaching assistant, entering a classroom full of other children who Miss Watson assured her would soon become her friends, and into first day of her education.

After what seemed a very, very long day, Ada was sitting yawning on the carpet while Mrs Bell, the teacher, read her new class a story. Then they heard an actual bell. It was a very abrupt sound and it made Ada jump. She wasn't the only one. Charlie Matheson began to cry. Miss Watson was quickly at his side.

"Well, children, you've done very well today," Mrs Bell said, "and I can tell we're going to have a wonderful year together. Thank you very much for your beautiful manners and behaving so well. I'm looking forward to seeing you all tomorrow. You will need to get your bags from your pegs, and your coats if you have them... hang on, hang on, in groups. Go in your table groups, beginning with Animals."

Ada looked to her right, where her new friend Clara was sitting. They grinned at each other. "Animals!" they whispered excitedly to each other. That was them.

"Come on," Miss Watson said, ushering them out.

And they stood and they walked very sensibly to the cloak room, as they had been primed to do, and took their bags off their pegs. On the way out, Clara clutched Ada's hand but then, seeing her mum waiting, she fled to her, not looking back. Ada saw Clara's mum swing her up into the air, smiling. She looked for Louisa but she didn't recognise any of the adults standing around.

She felt suddenly small and alone but then, "Ada!" she heard, and she saw her mum rushing across the playground.

"Thank God!" Louisa said, hugging Ada to her and looking apologetically to Miss Watson. "The tube stopped in the tunnel, and I thought I was going to be late, and..."

"You made it," Miss Watson smiled. "Bang on time. And Ada's had a great day, haven't you Ada?"

"Yes. Mum, I made an elephant with clay, and I wrote my name, and I got a friend called Clara, and..."

Louisa laughed, her eyes shining and her relief evident.

"That sounds wonderful," she said. "Thank you, Miss Watson." But the teaching assistant was already talking to somebody else's mum.

Louisa scooped her little girl up.

"Not here, Mummy!" Ada said. "We're at school."

"You're absolutely right. Sorry." Louisa put Ada back down. "May I hold your hand though?"

Ada considered this. "Yes."

"Should we get some sweets on the way home? To say well done for being so good on your first day?"

"Yes please."

And they walked, mother and daughter, hand in hand, out of the playground and along the busy road. The heat rose from the pavement and the queuing traffic coughed exhaust fumes into the humid air. Louisa was glad when they reached a corner where they turned away from the main road and into a street lined with tall townhouses and strong old trees, at the end of which was a convenience store where they could stop for a little paper bag of white chocolate buttons covered in hundreds and thousands – and a bottle of chilled white wine.

The day she had been dreading for months was over. Ada had enjoyed it. Louisa had made it to her meeting and she'd still got back to school in time to pick her daughter up. It had been a matter of principle that she should do so today, even if she never managed it again. Her daughter's first day at school. Tick. She had done it all by herself – well, she and Ada had done it together. A team of two. That's what they were and that's what they would always be.

Ada felt the warmth of her mum's gaze and, clutching her bag at the top so as not to melt the sweets inside, she skipped happily along, unaware that in the morning she would decide that actually she wasn't too keen on going to school every single day and would rather stay at home. But Louisa would have left for work by then and it would be down to Georgie, Ada's nanny (or 'childminder' as Louisa preferred to call her, as if that made any difference to anything) to fight that particular battle.

Ada

The music from the BBC series of *Pride and Prejudice* is running through my head as we turn off the road and onto the driveway that leads to Josh's family home. I used to watch *Pride and Prejudice* with Mum sometimes as it's one of her favourites, and if ever I hear the music it's immediately comforting and takes me back to evenings in, just the two of us. Mum would normally have done a bit of work, and I'd have finished my homework, then we'd have got a big bowl of popcorn and a drink each – milkshake for me, wine for her – and pulled the curtains closed against the outside world, curling up on the settee, the popcorn placed between us. I sometimes wish for those times again, particularly when I'm feeling a bit unsure of myself, as I am now.

When I try to imagine what Josh's house is going to look like, the words 'country pile' spring to mind, although that phrase has also often made me think of cow pats, which is not quite as romantic somehow.

I am in Josh's car, wedged into the back seat between Sasha and Pippa, while Archie is in the passenger seat and has taken over the stereo. He's obsessed with hip hop at the moment and looks slightly put out when Josh turns the music off.

"Won't Mummy and Daddy like it?" Archie asks.

"Don't be a dick, Archie," Sasha warns. "Or maybe Josh's mummy and daddy will kick you out."

"I just like to listen to the birds along here," Josh explains, not in the least offended by Archie. "Listen." He slows the car and opens his window. He's right, here on this driveway lined with huge horse chestnut and oak trees, the air is brimming with birdsong.

"That's lovely," I say. "Beats Public Enemy any day. Sorry, Archie."

"What?!" Archie turns and looks at me with mock annoyance. It gives me a secret thrill, which I try not to show. I am determined not to be just another member of the Archie Kingston fan club. But with him sitting so close to me, his mustard-coloured hoodie bringing out the colour of his deep brown eyes as he smiles at me, I am finding it hard to be anything else. I can feel my face turning red and I'm glad when he's turned back again. I busy myself fiddling with my phone, hoping that neither Sasha nor Pippa has noticed my flushed cheeks.

I am also keen to keep hidden the fact that I am feeling a little nervous, wondering if I might be a bit out of my depth in this situation. This is not my world, you see. My mum is a successful businesswoman, which I know sounds a bit naff, but it's meant that I have been able to keep up materially with the others, if necessary. But from all of our group of friends it is just me and Archie, and Jack – who is driving the other carload – who are not products of the English public school system and were not brought up in homes with multiple dogs and ponies and staff, and weekend shooting parties, and fine old names to uphold.

Josh, who I had originally known as Josh Bennion, has turned out to be Joshua James Hywel Ogilvy-Bennion. His grandfather was Welsh, and his grandmother Cornish. He told me this (although not that they occupied minor positions in the aristocracy) not long after we had first met, and it made me feel like we probably had something in common. Although my grandmother is not Cornish, having been born in London, she's lived in Cornwall most of her life and Cornwall holds a special place in my heart thanks to her. My mum actually is Cornish but she made the reverse journey and lived most of her life to date in London. It's only recently that she's moved back to Cornwall, hence my slightly up-in-the-air situation now. I have no home to return to.

When I eventually discovered Josh's full name, and that his father is Lord Ogilvy-Bennion, who has a seat in the House of Lords, I realised that we probably have a lot less in common than I had first imagined. But I couldn't tell Josh that; he'd be mortified. He goes to great lengths to hide these things away, but I don't think he should. He is who he is, and he can't help who his parents are, any more than anyone else can – including his parents.

There is beeping behind us and I turn to see Jack's face grinning at me from behind his windscreen. Rachael is waving from the passenger seat and Charlotte and Will are in the back seat, no doubt holding hands and gazing at each other lovingly. Honestly, if they weren't such lovely people, it would make you sick.

It's been interesting, getting to know these friends of mine, and hearing their take on the world. They're not at all keen on maintaining the status quo and for the most part my friends seem to carry a great deal of guilt. Charlotte's family, for instance, are known to have benefitted enormously from the slave trade in the 18th and 19th centuries. She's on track to become a barrister and incredibly keen to work on human rights cases. Will, meanwhile, wants to make his name in investigative journalism, particularly in the developing world. They share high ideals and want to make the world a better place, and they love each other deeply, as their regular public displays of affection remind us.

Sasha and Pippa are talking about creating an ethical clothing label ("Wonder where they're planning to get the funding for that," Archie said to me quietly once).

Josh, meanwhile, is just quietly keen to forge a career in something creative, and hopefully something that will benefit other people too, and to live life simply and well. He says he does not want the wealth or the lifestyle his parents have and is happy that his older brother Andrew will have to take the brunt of the expectations that come with being an Ogilvy-Bennion.

That's another thing which amazes me; the tradition of the oldest son still standing to inherit the lot: titles, land, responsibility. I mean, I know this is how it is in the royal family but apparently it's still a thing in the aristocracy in general. Mum is, not surprisingly, steadfastly against all of this stuff and maybe it's the thought of her that is setting me a bit on edge as well. Imagining my mum coming here and whether or not she'd be able to bite her tongue. Never mind my mum; imagine if it was my gran! She actually had to work at a manor house once, after the war. She was a governess, I think. She doesn't say a lot about that time but I gather it wasn't a very happy experience and I think it's left her feeling a bit antagonistic towards the upper classes. The *landed gentry* as she'd call them, sarcastically. She is not here though, I remind myself, and neither is Mum. It's just me, and I can be exactly who I want to be. I hope I can. I want to be myself.

Archie, Jack and I cannot claim to have wanted for much growing up but our healthy financial situations are the consequence of our parents' hard-won success. It seems that all of our parents came from less-than-well-off backgrounds and worked their way up ("Climbed the greasy pole," according to Archie, who seems to have a bit of an axe to grind with his dad) to where they are now. I hope this means that we do have one foot – or at least a toe – in the real world. And I don't feel ashamed, or guilty. In fact, I feel proud of how well Mum has done, and of the way that she has brought me up. I had a lovely home and we had great holidays, and we never had to worry about money, which I realise makes us incredibly fortunate, but I don't think I have been spoiled. I certainly hope not. I know not everybody is as lucky as me and I know a lot of people work very hard yet still struggle financially, but I think it's OK to be proud of my mum. Her life has not been easy.

Josh is moving the car forward again, and Jack is following close behind. I look around me, along the tree-lined avenue, and I can feel my heart beating a bit faster. I sit back, trying to relax. *They're just people*, I tell myself. *Just like everybody else.* And then the house swings into view and Archie turns to me and raises his eyebrows. It's huge! I have to count the number of windows along the front, and then count them again. There are eleven upstairs, and eight downstairs – four either side of a ridiculously big wooden door, which is guarded either side by grey stone sphinxes. This door opens slowly and then there she is, Lady Ogilvy-Bennion, or Mummy as Josh calls her occasionally, when he forgets he should just be saying Mum. She doesn't look like a Mum, to be fair. I mean, my mum is a bit forbidding, I imagine, if you don't know her. She can certainly do the scary work persona very well. Josh's mum, however, is in another league. She's tall and thin, with her hair scraped back into a bun, and today she is wearing riding clothes. When I say riding clothes, I mean of course an immaculate navy-blue fitted Burberry jacket, jodhpurs and boots.

Archie whistles. "Nice boots."

"Didn't I say not to be a dick, Archie?" Sasha hisses. She sits up straight, and when the car stops she opens the door and unfolds her long limbs gracefully as she steps out.

"Antonia!" she says, stepping forward to take Josh's mother's hands and kissing her on either cheek. Watching Sasha now, it's almost impossible to recognise that student I've spent the last three years with, who has devoted quite a lot of that time to smoking weed and frequenting illegal raves.

I follow Sasha out of the car, brushing crisp crumbs off my new linen trousers, annoyed to see that they have predictably creased up during the journey.

"Hello Ava," Josh's mum – Antonia – calls.

"Ada," Sasha corrects her, giving me a huge grin and rolling her eyes.

"Ada! I am so sorry." Not sorry enough not to cast her eyes up and down the length of me, I notice, but I am too keen to be accepted to find this annoying. And then I am annoyed at myself to be so eager to be accepted. *They're just people,* I tell myself again. I feel a hand touch my shoulder briefly and I almost flinch but I turn to see it is Josh. I smile at him and remind myself that this is his home, and that his parents can't be all that bad if they've managed to produce somebody as lovely as him. My best friend (after Clara of course), and my rock throughout uni, I am here because of him. When I remember that, I feel a little bit better.

Still, I flounder as I approach Josh's mother. "Hello Mrs... Lady..."

"Oh, do call me Antonia," she smiles at me and her face softens. I see Josh in her.

"Thank you," I say, although if I can possibly help it I won't have to call her anything. Josh has told us his parents are heading off to Monaco later today so it will be just the nine of us in an hour or two. If I can only manage not to make a fool of myself between now and then, I should be able to relax.

2013

"Can Clara come over after school?"

"You know it's not as easy as that," Louisa had sighed. "I won't be here, will I?"

"But Grace said she can look after us both."

"I don't know. I don't feel comfortable with it."

"You always say that."

"It's always true."

"But I'd prefer it if I was here."

"You never minded when it was Georgie."

"But Georgie is… family."

Georgie, who had been Ada's nanny and childminder since she was a baby, had met the 'love of her life', Adam (she said she knew it was a sign when his name was so similar to Ada's) and married him, and become pregnant, within one whirlwind year. Louisa had been bereft at her loss, as had Ada.

Now they had Grace, who was lovely but had a very large pair of boots to fill. It was not fair to compare the two women, Louisa knew that, but she couldn't help it, and she was not yet sure that she trusted Grace enough to allow her the responsibility of having somebody else's child as well as her own.

"I've got to work…"

"Clara's mum works."

"Well yes, but she only—" Louisa cut her sentence short. She didn't like what she'd been about to say. *She only does admin, and only works part-time.* The judgement was implied and entirely unfair. She liked Mary and knew that it had been her choice to put her career on the back-burner while her family were young.

Clara was the middle child of three, with an older brother, Harry, and a younger sister, Lily. "I should have stuck with just one," Mary had joked to Louisa quietly when she had come to collect Ada after a sleepover.

This was Louisa's concession; on weekends, Clara could come, and she could stay as long as she wanted to. She was no bother and Louisa loved hearing the sound of the girls giggling together. It also meant she could get on with some work with no (or minimal) guilt.

"I worry Ada's lonely, though," Louisa had admitted. It was not something she would have told many people, not wanting to show any weakness. Even with her own mum, she pretended her life was exactly as she had planned it.

"Oh, she's grand." Mary was easy-going and grounded when it came to children and parenting. It helped Louisa greatly, easing her anxieties and self-doubt. Mary put her hand on Louisa's arm. "She's got you, hasn't she? And she and Clara are thick as thieves. Ada's always welcome at our place, you know. Honestly. She just slots in with us all."

Louisa had liked the thought of this, that against all odds she was raising a daughter who was easy-going and adaptable.

"Actually," Mary said, "we were wondering if maybe Ada would like to come on holiday with us in the summer. A little celebration for the girls finishing school."

"Can I, Mum? Can I?" Ada, who had seemed to be engrossed in the film she and Clara were watching, had turned round, pulling a lolly out of her mouth to make her plea. Her lips and tongue were stained dark purple from whatever awful substance the lolly was made of. Louisa and Mary both laughed.

"Please say she can! Please! We'll be really well behaved and help with the washing up and everything," Clara added her own entreaties via a blue-tinged mouth.

"Well…" Louisa had looked at the pair of them; her own, beautiful, sunny-natured daughter and her equally beautiful, sunny-natured friend. They could be sisters, she thought; cousins, at the very least. They were certainly close enough. "I don't see why not. And maybe next year," she said, already doubting if this was a good idea but committed to it now that the words were coming out of her mouth, "I could take you both to Cornwall?"

"To see Gran?" Ada asked excitedly.

"Yes, of course."

"Yes, yes, yes!" Ada had exclaimed, and the two girls had squealed excitedly, hugging each other.

Really, thought Louisa, if it was that easy to make them happy, how could it be anything but a good idea?

Louisa reminded her daughter of this now. "Look, I know it seems unfair, and I am sorry I'm not here more but remember Clara has two parents who work, and Mary is home a lot more than I am."

"I know, Mum," Ada had sighed.

"You can always ask Clara round at the weekend."

"She's going to her uncle's at the weekend. They're having a family party." Ada pouted. "I wish we had a big family like them."

"Do you?"

"Yes, Clara's got loads of cousins, and they're really fun. They make potions together and throw them at people walking by."

Louisa raised her eyebrows at this.

"I mean, not really *at* people. It's just the bathroom window's over the street and they accidentally dropped some out once, and…"

"Hmm," Louisa had smiled. "Maybe it's not such a bad thing you don't have cousins, they sound like a bad influence!"

"They're not," Ada said, outraged. "Just fun. I wish Uncle Laurie had kids."

"But even if he did, they'd be all the way up in Scotland. Come on, I tell you what, if Clara's not around, why don't we go shopping on Saturday? We can start to look for some things for your holiday. And we can have lunch too."

"Really? At Bocca?"

"If you like." Louisa had smiled at the turnaround of Ada's mood. If only it was as easy to sort herself out sometimes. Still, she'd enjoy her day out with Ada as much as her daughter would. She would do anything for her girl and the thought of Ada going away for a week without her in the summer made her stomach twist slightly. What would she do without her? The answer was obvious: work.

Ada

"Josh, why don't you show your friends to their rooms, darling?" Antonia asks sweetly and I try not to react when Archie whispers into my ear, "Don't they have a butler for that kind of thing?"

Josh, always sharp, flashes a glance our way. He knows what Archie is like but I wonder if he is feeling a bit more sensitive; defensive, even. This is his (enormous) home and his family, after all. Don't most of us feel more protective when it comes to these things?

I just smile openly at Josh and I lift my bag from the floor.

"Oh no, Ava – Ada – you're not to carry your bags up. Josh can do this, and I'll see if Andrew is around, too."

"Is Andy here this weekend as well?" Sasha asks innocently. I can see right through her. She's got a thing for Josh's older brother, I know it.

"Yes, that's right. We have to have at least one responsible adult with you lot around, haven't we? What was that, Joshua?"

Josh had coughed into his hand at his mother's words. "Nothing. Just something in my throat."

Saving him from further explanation, and as if he's heard his name, Josh's older brother comes swanning into the room. He is dressed in tight jeans and a checked, expensive-looking shirt. "Hello students!" he greets us.

"Not anymore," Sasha says, never backwards in coming forwards.

"Oh that's right, of course. This is your end of uni celebration isn't it? What a coincidence you've chosen a weekend when the folks are away. Don't worry Mummy, I'll keep an eye on them all."

I can't help but notice his eyes are already on Sasha as he says this.

"Thank you darling," Antonia says, "now be a love and help these girls with their bags, will you?"

"Of course." Andrew smoothly lifts Sasha's and Pippa's bags. "Follow me, ladies."

He seems not to have noticed that there are three other 'ladies' here, also with bags, and it seems Antonia is no longer interested either. While Andrew leads the way, Sasha and Pippa trotting obediently after him and hanging off his every word, Josh picks up his own bag and mine, while Jack takes his and Rachael's. Charlotte, meanwhile, has not put her bag down, and refuses Will's help. "I can manage thank you!"

"I know you can," he replies, and they smile at each other.

With Josh leading this second contingent, Archie striding alongside him, I follow on behind the others, taking my time to look around. The house smells of polish and there is a very faint scent of woodsmoke on the air. Josh has told me that even in the height of summer the family might have a fire going; the house is so big and dark that it can feel cold inside, even when outside it's sweltering. On a table at the bottom of the staircase there is a photo of Josh's dad shaking hands with David Cameron. Next to it, another picture – of some red-coated men and women on horseback, gathered in a pub car park on a cold winter's day.

I shudder inwardly but I remind myself that I am a guest here, that I should not be being so judgey, and that this is not who Josh is anyway. We are not all products of our upbringing – or if we are, sometimes it's a case of objecting, rebelling and going the opposite way.

"Ada, you're in here," Josh says to me, opening the door to a vast room with views across the gardens to the hills beyond. He deposits my bag on the four-poster bed.

"Wow!" I say, and Josh looks embarrassed. The others have wandered in too and Archie is raising his eyebrows at me from behind Josh's back. I ignore him. "It's lovely, Josh," I say. "And that view is amazing."

"This is my favourite room," he tells me. "I knew you'd like it."

"Thank you," I smile.

"You're sharing a bathroom with Rachael – it's just across the corridor – come and have a look and I'll show the others where they're staying."

Imagine having enough spare rooms to host a cohort of eight extra people! While Will and Charlotte are sharing, that still means that there must be at least seven spare rooms. Very possibly more. The family sleep at the west side of the house and the guest rooms are to the east. Imagine having a house that you can separate into west and east! I think of Gran's little terraced house with its three small bedrooms and the attic where she used to paint, before her legs got too old and creaky to get up and down the ladder. I picture her cosy living room, where she sits in the window and watches the world go by – and her kitchen where she and I used to make jam tarts, and the little garden with the vegetable patch. Oh but I love it there, so much. I feel a little contraction of my heart at the thought of it and once more my stomach turns over as I wonder if I really am out of my depth here.

It's only two days, I tell myself. And once Josh's parents are out of the way, I'll feel more like me. Except I hadn't known Andrew was going to be here, and his presence is putting me on edge. I've only met him once before, when he dropped by to visit Josh on his way back from 'the City' and, if I'm honest, I'm a bit scared of him. I have no idea what Sasha sees in him, even if he is quite good-looking. Maybe she likes his self-assuredness. To me, it comes across as over-confidence; arrogance, even, but maybe in their world this is just how people are. They are not brought up to doubt themselves.

"I'll just use the bathroom," I say, as the others go on to be shown their rooms. I'm grateful for the chance for a few moments by myself, although disconcerted that there is no lock on the door. Do rich people not have any need for privacy? At least it's only Rachael that I'm sharing with.

My god, even the bathroom has a view! The vast window looks across the yard at the back of the house, which is surrounded by stables and outbuildings, all joined together in a neat oblong, with a gap at the other side where presumably deliveries can be made, horses can go in and out, etc. I do honestly feel like I am in *Pride and Prejudice*, although I bet to the Darcies of this world the Ogilvy-Bennions would still count as poor relations. Thank God Josh doesn't have any evil sisters to cast aspersions on me. Not that I'm casting myself as Lizzie, by the way. I just know that I'd be easy prey for women like that.

I use the loo then look in the mirror. I see that as well as the crisp crumbs and creased trousers, I am also sporting slightly smudged mascara. Why does this matter? I know it doesn't, but I really want to be able to stand my ground. I don't want to give Josh's family any reason to look down on me and yes, I know they have given me no reason to think that they are doing that (although it would be nice if his mum got my name right), and very possibly the problem here lies with me, not them. Perhaps I've just got a chip on my shoulder, as Gran would put it.

I go back to my room and sit on the bed, then lie back fully. It's extremely comfortable and smells of freshly laundered linen. My head brushes something and I turn to see there is a teddy and an envelope on the pillow. I open the envelope and pull out a card which also has a teddy on the front of it.

Inside it reads: *Congratulations on completing your studies. We hope you have a wonderful weekend. Please make yourself at home. Antonia and Jamie.*

I can't help but smile at this and I feel bad, for my antagonism and defensiveness.

There's a knock on the door.

"Hello?" I sit up.

The door opens and Archie comes in. I sit up straighter.

"You alright?" he asks.

"Yes!" I laugh, brandishing the teddy.

"I got a bottle of whisky," he grins.

"Bloody hell!"

24

"I know. Josh said we should all meet downstairs in half an hour but I wondered if you want to come and explore with me first?"

"Do you think we should? Isn't it a bit weird to go wandering round somebody else's house?"

"I was thinking of the garden... sorry, the grounds," he says, pulling a neatly rolled joint from his pocket and grinning.

"Maybe later?" I suggest, thinking of Josh's parents.

"Come on," Archie pleads. "It's party time, isn't it?"

"What if Antonia catches us... or Jamie?"

"I'm pretty sure we can find somewhere to hide in their three hundred acres."

His brown eyes are on mine and I don't really see how I can resist. "Well, I'll come with you to have a look around. Let's just see about the... smoke. I don't want to upset Josh. But I suppose it can't hurt to explore."

"Hooray!" he grins and I feel pathetically pleased. "Let's go!"

I keep an eye out for Josh's parents, or brother, or the gardener, as we head out of the front of the house and across the gravel driveway. There are rhododendrons bursting out all around us and the air is filled with the scent of flowers. Up above, three buzzards glide in circles around each other, emitting their high-pitched cries. I breathe in deeply and feel something indefinable. It is to do with the freshness and clarity of the air. This place is so still, and so open, and it feels very different to the heavy, humid atmosphere in the city where I grew up, laden with exhaust and smoke and vape fumes. There, the sounds of traffic and building work are the constant backing track, seasoned with sirens and loud stereos pumping out music. Even by the sea, where the salty breeze blows clean air in from across the waves, it is not this still, and there is constant change, with the fluctuating tide, and the coming and going of holidaymakers. Here, it is calm, and tranquil, and so green, and it feels as though it has been this way for hundreds of years. I suppose it probably has.

"Have you seen the lake?" Archie asks.

"There's a lake?"

"Of course there is! No self-respecting country family would be seen dead without their own lake!"

"Wow."

"I know. And to think the kids at school called me posh! Just because Mum and Dad have got nice cars and we once went on a holiday to Bali."

"It's all scalable, isn't it?"

"I like that. Yes, it is. I feel like a commoner here."

"I know what you mean."

"Let's stick together, shall we?"

I don't reply, although I can think of nothing I'd like more.

We step around behind the house, emerging onto a walled patio, beyond which are sloping gardens leading down to the lake. Josh's family lake! I laugh.

"Crazy, isn't it? All of this for one family."

"Yeah. It's a bit mental."

"A bit? It's completely wrong."

"But Josh would say the same, wouldn't he?" I feel protective of my friend. "And besides, we didn't have to accept their invitation."

"Oh I know, it's not them that I've got a problem with

– not really. They were born into this. It's more that this is the way the world works. Society, anyway. How are there so many hundreds of homeless people, and thousands of kids whose families can't even afford to give them breakfast, when there are also a tiny number of people with this–" he opens his arms – "excess?"

"I say, who let the Bolshies in?" We both jump at a voice coming from behind us. I turn to see Josh's dad – Jamie – grinning at us.

"I take your point Archibald, I really do," he says, stepping forward to shake Archie's hand, and then offering me a kiss on the cheek. "Ada," he says. "Lovely to see you again."

He's a charming one, Josh's dad. I've met him twice before, and he's always been exceedingly polite and asked interested questions about my studies and my artwork, and even my mum. Somewhere along the line, at some charity auction or something, their paths have crossed, and he remembers her fondly, or so he says.

I realise Archie is tongue-tied. I hadn't expected that.

"Hello sir…"

"Jamie," Josh's dad says, mock-sternly.

"Jamie. Thank you for letting us come to stay."

"It's our pleasure. I'm sorry we're having to jet off but I'm sure you won't miss us. Just don't go too wild, alright?" He looks at me. "I remember all too well what it's like being your age."

I smile, wanting to reassure him that we are actually all incredibly sensible but then I see that Archie has the joint tucked behind his ear. What on earth possessed him to do that? I try to catch his eye and he looks at me, puzzled. I widen my eyes and I touch my ear.

It takes a moment but he catches my drift and raises his hand to his head.

"Your lake is beautiful," I say to Jamie, hoping to take his attention that way. It works, and out of the corner of my eye I see Archie removing the offending article and depositing it in the front pouch of his hoodie.

"Yes, I like it," says Jamie. "My grandfather had it lengthened when he bought this place, after he'd escaped the homeland. Wales, you know."

"Yes, Josh said your dad – father – was Welsh. And your mother's Cornish?"

"Correct. I believe we have that in common," Jamie says. "Anyway, I won't hold you up. I've a case to pack and I believe you have a joint to smoke. I'd recommend the boathouse for that. You can watch the wildlife and the reflections of the clouds on the water. Just don't fall in, and don't upset the swans."

"I… I—" says Archie.

"I told you," Jamie lays a hand on his shoulder, "I remember what it's like being your age."

He smiles at us both and turns on his heel.

"Bloody hell!" says Archie. "I thought we'd got away with it."

"I don't think he cares, to be honest."

"No, well these toffs don't. They just do what they like. You know, when our grandparents and great-grandparents were being brought up to be good, god-fearing and chaste, this lot were sleeping around, having affairs with each other's wives, or shagging the servants. It was expected of them."

"Come on!" I laugh. "Maybe that's enough of the class-bashing for now. They are just people, like us."

"Not quite like us."

"No, but anyway... are we going to smoke this spliff?"

Something about that conversation with Jamie has sparked me into life and I feel suddenly carefree and like I want very much to celebrate everything. We are young, and we've worked bloody hard, and just for this brief spell of time we have no responsibilities. Every now and then in these last few weeks, I've had this brief glimpse of something, the world opening up before me, with all its possibilities. Now, like the sun breaking out from behind a cloud, it swings fully into view and I'm flooded with light.

"Race you!" I say, and I'm tearing down the slope, through the gardens and down the little walkway to the boathouse.

Archie catches up with me, his arm snaking around my waist. "You cheated!" he says, gasping, laying his head on my shoulder. "That was a false start."

"Sure," I grin, pretending it's the most natural thing in the world to have this boy so close to me, his arm around me and his breath warm and rapid against my skin.

I don't know what to do next and I'm grateful that he takes my hand and pulls me down next to him so we are sitting on the little pontoon, resting against the wooden boards of the boathouse. He takes the joint from his pocket, straightening it out, then he lights the little twist of paper at the end and takes a long, deep draw. The smoke smells strong against the fresh country air but it's not unpleasant. I'm not much of a smoker to be honest. Today, though, I want to throw caution to the wind. I take the joint from Archie when he offers it and I put it between my lips, inhaling. I'm aware that Archie's eyes are on me but I don't look at him. Instead, I studiously gaze across the water, where lily pads mingle with pond skaters and other little insects which dart about the surface and just above the water. Swallows perform little aerobatic displays, swooping low in across the water, soft white bellies nearly skimming the lake. At the other side of the water, a mother duck swims, followed by her little brood of ridiculously cute fluffy ducklings.

I sigh.

"Alright?" Archie asks.

"Yes," I say, exhaling smoke and trying not to cough. "Here. I won't have much more. Thanks, though."

"Pleasure." He puts the joint in his mouth and shuffles closer to me, leans his head against mine. "This is pretty perfect, isn't it?"

Yes, I think, *it is.* And I close my eyes, trying to imprint this moment in time on my mind, to look back on when I'm old and grey, or just when I'm sitting in an office on a cold winter's day. I like to do this sometimes; create a little index of memories I can flick back through and draw some comfort from when I'm not feeling so happy.

"Look at that!" Archie says and I open my eyes to see a full-grown dragonfly darting around in front of us, flashing green and blue through the air as it shows itself off. Beyond, a swan sails into view. Archie stubs out the joint. "I think I've had enough too, for now," he says, and he puts his arm around me. I lean against him, barely able to believe that all those long months of studying and working late are over and now here I am, with Archie Kingston of all people, sitting in the boathouse of the country manor we are sharing with our friends all weekend.

Yes, I think again. *This really is pretty perfect.*

2013

On the way to Devon, Ada sat in the back row of the people-carrier, she and Clara sandwiching five-year-old Lily. In front of them were Clara's brother Harry and his friend Daniel, who Clara had a crush on. Ada didn't dare tell her friend that she had similar feelings for Harry.

The boys were already two years into secondary school and seemed so grown up. Daniel, who was very dark-skinned and tall, even had to shave, according to Clara. How she knew, Ada had no idea, but the thought of what other changes that might mean were happening to him physically made her feel quite strange.

Although she had known Harry for years and in their younger days they'd all mucked about together at soft-play places, and made dens in Clara's living room, these days Ada found herself a bit tongue-tied around him. She was not used to boys; not men, either. Really, it was just Clara's dad, Andy, and her own uncle, Laurie, who she had anything to do with. She had not even had any male teachers throughout primary school, though that was all set to change.

The thought of secondary school, with its hundreds of children and its long, unforgiving corridors which she was sure she would get lost in, was terrifying.

"We could look at somewhere smaller," her mum had told her, naming a couple of the local independent schools, but Ada knew that while they could afford it, these were not really what her mum wanted for her. In fact, they'd had a frank discussion, where Louisa had told her that she wanted it to be Ada's choice but had gone on to list the reasons for going to a state school, chief among them that they would offer a greater mix of people and be more reflective of the real world.

"You'll do well whatever, Ada, I know you will. But if you really want to, we can go and look around St Teresa's."

This was an all-girls' school and Ada knew her gran had gone somewhere similar, and that was how she had ended up in Cornwall, when the school was evacuated there during the war.

"Did you like it, Gran?" she asked Elise during one of their weekly phone calls. Ada wanted to gather the facts before she made a decision.

"I loved it!" Elise said. "Or at least I did in many ways. But I was terrified of it at first, and of leaving Mum, because of course I was to be a boarder too. At least you'd be going home every night."

"But what about it being only girls?"

"Well, I don't know. I suppose I didn't know any different. In those days, even at primary school we were separated, with different entrances for girls and boys. Different playgrounds, too."

"Really?" It was hard for Ada to imagine not having everyone in together. She thought of Charlie Matheson, who would play with the girls more than the boys. What would he have done, in an all-boys' playground?

"Of course I had Violet with me, and she made all the difference."

"She was your best friend?"

"She was, back then. I'm ashamed to say we lost touch, though, over the years. I don't know what happened to Violet but she was a very clever girl. I am quite sure she went on to do great things."

"And you went on to work at Tregynon Manor?" Ada asked.

"Well, yes, for a while. And only in a very small way. I was a governess."

"For two boys and a girl?"

"Two brothers and their little sister," Elise confirmed.

"And they all learned together?"

"Well actually, no. Not always. The boys were taken off to do riding and other sports on a Wednesday afternoon, and I would have Tabitha all to myself. We'd go for walks, and collect shells, and study wildlife…"

"So she had to do all the boring stuff!" Ada said, outraged. She was beginning to cotton on to the idea of gender inequality and keen to identify it in as many places as possible.

"Well," her gran had laughed, "I don't like to think of it like that. Hopefully I made it interesting. And fun."

"But she wasn't allowed to go riding because she was a girl!"

"Maybe," Elise mused, "but perhaps because of her age as well. I remember teaching her to swim, so she wasn't held back. And actually, do you know, I remember her father telling me he wanted her to be just as good and well educated as her brothers… and to go on and do great things in her life."

"Oh." Ada was pulled up at this thought. "And did she?"

"Well, I'm afraid I don't know. Because I wasn't with them for long."

"That's sad."

"It is. I was quite attached to them, the children."

"So you lost touch with Violet and with the children you looked after?"

"Yes, I was quite careless, wasn't I?" Ada thought her gran sounded a bit sad. "But then I met Maudie, when I started work at Fawcett's, and I have been very careful not to lose her. She and I are friends for life."

Ada had met Maudie, who lived in a big white house with huge gardens overlooking the sea. Her husband Fred had died quite a long time ago. Maudie had a sports car, which she sometimes gave Ada a ride in, roof down and wind whipping through their hair. She also had a little field next to her garden, where she kept two donkeys that she'd rescued. Ada loved going to visit her and she could see how happy her gran was when she was with her friend.

"I think I know what I'm going to do."

"Oh yes?"

"Yes. I'm going to go to the same school as Clara. She's my best friend and I want to be with her."

If she was really honest, Ada was also finding her head filling more with the idea of boys and romance. She'd been to visit Georgie and Adam and their baby Arthur a number of times and she could see the way Georgie laughed at Adam's jokes, and how her eyes sparkled when she looked at him. Ada also liked to observe the relationship between Clara's parents, Mary and Andy, who teased each other and sometimes pretended they didn't like each other but held hands when they were out walking round National Trust places or even down the local high street. And sometimes in the evening they'd sit snuggled together, watching a film.

"Urgh!" Clara and Harry would say if their parents happened to kiss in front of them but Ada found it fascinating, not having any examples of romantic relationships in her immediate family. Her dad was never even mentioned by her mum, having been explained away as a 'necessity but not a consideration in our lives'. Her grandad had died when her mum was a baby and her gran had never remarried. Uncle Laurie lived with a lady called Liz but apparently that was for work, which was a bit confusing.

When she was little, Ada had not questioned any of this but these days she was beginning to think she might like a relationship of her own one day. If she went to an all-girls' school that was going to be difficult, because she was already sure she didn't like girls in that way. No, she had made up her mind. It was going to have to be a mixed school. And she wasn't being dishonest because she really didn't want to be separated from Clara either. The boys were just going to be a bonus.

"Well that's one thing to consider," Elise said, smiling at her granddaughter's reasoning, and sympathising with her wanting to stay with her friend. "But maybe you should talk it over with your mum." Too late, she realised that her talk of Violet and Tabitha was helping to shape Ada's decision. She just hoped that Louisa wouldn't mind.

Ada

"Alright?" Josh asks me when I return. Archie has nipped back to his room for something so I arrive in the kitchen alone, pink-cheeked and smiling, to find my friend placing a kettle on top of the Aga.

"Yes, great!" I smile and hug him. "Thank you so much for this, Josh. For inviting us all here, I mean."

"It's my pleasure. Honestly, I wasn't sure about it at first, I know it's a bit…"

"Big?" I suggest.

He laughs. "I wasn't going to say that, but you're right, it is a bit big. I was going to say it's a bit of a pain having Andrew here."

"Well, it is his home."

"Yes, he's probably keeping an eye on his inheritance," Josh says sardonically.

"It's fine." I rub his arm. "I'm sure he's not going to want to hang out with all of us youngsters anyway."

"How old do you think he is?" Josh raises his eyebrows.

"Erm… maybe early thirties?" I hazard a guess.

Josh splutters. "He's only twenty-five. Three years older than me."

"But he's so… grown up."

"Well, he likes to give that impression anyway.

36

Especially around Mum and Dad. And attractive young women too."

"Like Sasha? And Pippa?"

"I like the way you don't consider yourself in that number, Ada, but you must know you're a bit of a catch as well."

"A bit of a catch? I don't think so. If this was *Pride and Prejudice*, I'd be Lizzie's friend – what's her name? The one who ends up marrying Mr Collins."

"A very sensible match," Josh says. "I think of you as more of a Lydia though."

"Hey!" I swipe at his arm. "That's enough of your cheek. I think you're probably a Mr Bennett. No, scrub that. You're Mrs Bennett."

"So I'm a middle-aged hysterical woman? Thanks, Ava. At least I know where I stand with you."

"No offence," I grin, just as the kettle starts to whistle. "Don't you need to call your woman – Hill, isn't it? – to come and brew up?"

In truth, Josh is a bit of an enigma, at least where his romantic tendencies lie. I initially assumed he was gay, based admittedly on some fairly weak ideas about him being quite in touch with his feminine side, having lots of female friends, and he's very arty and always well turned out. In all the time I've known him though, he's never had a boyfriend, or girlfriend, or even a romantic encounter, or at least not one he's told me about.

Josh is the archetypal 'gay best friend' but I just don't know if he is actually gay. We clicked immediately, during a tutorial discussion, realised we lived close to each other, and he walked me back to my place, where I invited him in for dinner. He nipped out to get a bottle of white wine and some tomatoes and mozzarella (this was before he became vegan), and a handful of fresh basil from his own plant, and he showed me how to make Italian flatbreads and caprese salad. We turned up the radio and sang along to the songs we knew, drinking the wine and working side by side.

Since then, we've been almost inseparable. We chose most of the same modules on our course, regularly went to the cinema and ate out at local restaurants on student discount nights; we've been on cookery courses together, and last year we went to Italy on a residential art retreat. Mum loves him, and later this summer he's going to come and see me in Cornwall.

Josh has always been a confidante, and a shoulder to cry on when I've needed it, which has been quite a few times given my pathetic attempts at a love life, and my tendency to begin art projects only to reject them dramatically when they don't turn out how I'd like them to. Yet despite our closeness, Josh is not what I would call an open book. He probably knows more about me than I do about him. In fact, I know he does. And I also know that the more I prod him, the more closed he becomes, so I've learned to leave him to it and not to push him.

Sasha thinks he's still finding his feet – "He may even be asexual," she said knowledgably, "but I hope his brother isn't."

I'd rolled my eyes but I do love her. I just wonder how our friendship will progress once we're living different lives. In fact, I wonder that about a lot of my uni friendships. I can see Sasha getting sucked back into her world, and me into mine. Pippa and Sasha are old friends from school, so I know they'll stay in touch with each other, even if they never do get round to starting their ethical clothing company. Will and Charlotte have already decided to move in together in London so that they can be together but also in the heart of things to further their careers. Of course, their flat is one of Will's parents' 'portfolio' – "Doesn't your mum have a property portfolio?" Archie had asked me with a wicked glint in his eye – and I don't think they are going to struggle too much to live and eat in the world's fourth most expensive city. Jack and Rachael, I think, will stay in touch with each other at least. I'm watching them this weekend, in fact, as I have a suspicion they're interested in each other, though neither has said as much to me. I suppose I have the most in common with Josh and Archie, in terms of our love of art and also having little idea of what we want to do next.

Time will tell, whether our tight-knit group of friends will last the distance. I love to think that this time next year we could all be meeting up again, and each year well into the future.

We could bring in partners and eventually children, and dogs, and... I see a little future scene playing out with us all meeting here at Josh's parents' place. The sun is shining, of course, and there are picnic blankets laid out on the lawn where we adults sit smiling and chatting and drinking wine, while our offspring and pets chase each other around the beautifully landscaped gardens. Of course in reality, this place will at some point be Andrew's and he'd probably tell us to piss off. Still, I can dream...

One by one (well, two by two in the case of Will and Charlotte, and Jack and Rachael – told you!) the others join us in the kitchen and Josh pours tea from a huge pot.

Antonia appears. "We'll be setting off soon so I just wanted to say I hope you all have a lovely weekend and don't get too drunk!" She laughs. "Speaking of which, did you get your gifts, you boys?"

"Yes, thank you, Mrs – Antonia," Archie says very politely and Jack and Will offer their thanks, too.

"That's Jamie's favourite whisky so I hope you'll enjoy it."

"Thank you for my perfume too, Antonia," Sasha says. "It's gorgeous."

"Yes well I like that one, too."

"Yes, thank you so much," Pippa says, "that was lovely of you."

"Thank you for my gift as well," I say, not wanting to say I've got a teddy. At the back of my mind I'm wondering why I have been given a soft toy when everyone else seems to have been given very grown-up and I expect expensive presents. I can't help feeling like mine was a last-minute thing. Had they overlooked the fact that I was coming? Am I that insignificant?

Stop being paranoid, I caution myself. *You're reading far too much into this. It's nice to have been given anything. Now just stop it, and try and enjoy yourself!*

With a hug and a kiss for Josh, Antonia is gone. She brushes past me as she leaves. "Sorry Ava… Ada," she corrects herself.

Well, if there is some kind of problem – if I'm not up to scratch because my family aren't lords and ladies and we don't own half of Buckinghamshire – it's all the more reason for me to push myself harder. Work out what I want to do, and make a success of my life.

But just for now, as Archie reminds me, once we've heard Jamie shout his goodbyes, and the heavy wooden door slam shut... "Now, we party!"

After we finish our cups of tea.

We head out onto the lawn at the front of the house. Before us is the enormous gravel driveway and on the other side of that is a field with a horse and a Shetland pony. They whinny at us, trotting to the fence, and I watch them from a distance while Rachael and Charlotte go across to see them.

"Not a horsey type?" Josh asks, nudging me.

"What? No, they're beautiful, but I don't really know what to do with horses."

"Most of us have grown up on them," Sasha says. "I mean, it's just what you do at the weekend. I think I was on my first pony when I was three. Maybe even younger."

"I definitely had a go on a donkey, at the beach," I say, and am gratified by Archie's laughter.

"There's no way Louisa would have taken you on that kind of holiday!" Josh says. "And I know there are no donkeys on the beach where your gran lives."

"No, you're right. I've never actually been on a donkey, or a horse, apart from on a carousel in France. That was pretty well behaved, though it kept going round in circles."

"You, Ada, are an idiot," says Josh, popping open a bottle of wine. "Now who wants a glass of this?"

As it turns out, we all do, and so do Rachael and Charlotte when they return from petting the horse and pony, so Josh is soon opening another bottle, and then Archie's getting out a joint to smoke, and we are all soon settling back into our comfortable friendship.

The clouds which had blanketed the sky have begun to move off, allowing the warming sunlight to fall across the grass and onto us. I lie back, leaning my head against Josh, who tucks a daisy into my hair. With his parents out of the way and his brother nowhere to be seen, I relax and gaze up at the sky, watching a small gang of birds flit across the wide expanse of blue, and the last of the clouds clear away.

2013

When they finally arrived at their destination, everyone was extremely pleased to escape the confines of the car. They'd been stuck in traffic since Weston-super-Mare and at first Mary and Andy had attempted to keep everyone's spirits up with games of I Spy (ironically of course, for the teenagers and pre-teens, and frustratingly for Lily who was struggling with her letters) but eventually the heat of the day and the relentlessly long, slow lines of cars frayed their tempers. They fell out when Andy took a wrong exit off a roundabout near Bovey Tracey and had to turn around in the car park of the House of Marbles. Eventually, three hours after they'd hoped to be there, they reached their destination: a caravan park on the edge of Dartmoor.

"Bagsy top bunk!" Daniel had said, and Clara and Ada had just watched him in admiration as he forged his way into the boys' bedroom, which really was little more than a cupboard, with slim bunk beds, a wardrobe and a window.

"Whatever," said Harry, shrugging, swinging his own bag onto the bottom bunk. "It'll be hotter up there anyway." He turned to Ada and grinned and she felt her face turn a deep, unforgiving red.

Harry had already turned back to his bunk so he didn't notice but it seemed that Mary might have. She just smiled at Ada. "Come on, the girls' room is this way."

Ada and Clara were to share a double bed, with Lily tucked into a higher bunk which folded down from the wall. She was immediately enraptured, climbing up and down the ladder until Clara told her to stop.

"You can't be doing that all night, me and Ada need our sleep."

"Beauty sleep!" Harry called.

"I heard that."

"You were meant to."

"Where are you sleeping, Mum?"

"Ah, well, me and your dad will have the fold-down bed in the living area."

"What? Let me see!"

They trooped out and Mary showed them how the table transformed into a bed.

"Can't we sleep here?" Clara asked. "And you have the double bed? You deserve it, you and Dad."

Mary smiled. "I can see right through you, young lady. You don't want to share with your sister."

"It's not that…"

"Oh really?" Mary looked at Andy. "What do you think?"

"I don't know. I don't mind, really."

"We just thought we'd be the last ones up so it made sense for us to be out here."

"Mu-um, I'll be twelve in September. We're not going to bed early."

"But Ada's only just turned eleven."

"Yeah, but Ada's really grown-up. Her mum lets her stay up till whenever, doesn't she Ada?"

"Really?" Mary, who believed wholeheartedly in the benefits of a good night-time routine – perhaps largely because it was the only way she could ever have five minutes to herself – looked at Ada.

"Well, sort of. I mean, I don't have a bedtime, but I don't stay up really late." Ada was keen not to have her mum's reputation besmirched.

"Well you're very sensible. Unlike some people." Andy looked mock-sternly at Clara.

"We'll be fine. Honest. And then we can watch TV in bed," Clara whispered this last line to Ada.

"Go on then!" Mary said.

"Yes! Thanks Mum, you're the best."

The first night, all seven of them went to the onsite restaurant and bar, where there was live entertainment in the form of a singer, and then a disco.

After a while, Lily began to cry. "She's really tired," Mary said. "Come on, we'd better go back after these drinks."

"We can stay though, can't we Mum?" asked Harry.

"Well, I suppose so." Mary looked at her watch. "No later than half nine, though. OK?"

"What?"

"Half nine or you come back with us."

"OK."

"Can we stay too, Mum? Please?" wheedled Clara. "It's only a few minutes away from the caravan."

Mary looked at Andy. He was relaxed after his third pint and he just shrugged. "The boys'll be here."

"Well OK, but you two I want back by nine, OK?"

"Why don't they come back with us?" asked Daniel. "That way we can all walk back together."

Ada could sense Clara's excitement at this idea but she knew her friend was trying to act cool, like she didn't mind either way.

"Well, alright then," Mary said. "I'll check with your mum first, Ada, but if she doesn't mind then I think that should be OK."

Back in London, Louisa – distracted by work and a couple of glasses of wine down – didn't have a problem with anything, so it was fixed.

After ten minutes or so, Andy and Mary left with Lily, who was clinging onto her dad, her head on his shoulder. Without them there it suddenly all felt a bit awkward.

"I'll get us some drinks," Harry said, brandishing the twenty-pound-note Andy had left with him.

"And some crisps!" Clara said. "I mean, if you want some."

"Come and help will you, Dan?"

And as the two thirteen-year-olds walked to the bar, Clara turned to Ada. "Does my hair look a mess? Have I got anything between my teeth?"

"No, and no!" Ada laughed, and she noticed Clara move her chair closer to Daniel's so that by the time he returned, clutching four bags of crisps and a glass of Coke, they were practically touching. He moved his chair away slightly but Clara didn't seem to notice.

"Fancy a game of table football?" Harry asked Daniel, placing the three other glasses down on the table.

"Can we play too? Doubles?" asked Clara.

"Go on, then."

And that was what broke the ice. The four of them ignored the disco for the most part and spent what was left of Andy's money on table football, darts and crazy golf, which they finished just as it was getting dark.

"Shit!" Harry said, looking at his watch. "It's nearly half past!"

"Chill," said Daniel.

"Yeah, chill!" giggled Clara who, if Ada didn't know better, appeared to have been drinking.

"Come on," Harry said, and Ada obediently followed him, trying to match his pace. Daniel and Clara followed on behind.

Ada and Harry reached the caravan just two minutes late. "Sorry!" Harry said to his parents, out of breath. "We just had to finish crazy golf."

"I won!" Ada said, unable to help herself.

Harry grinned and nudged her. "Show-off."

"Ssh!" Mary said, though she was smiling. "Lily's only just gone to sleep. Over-tired," she explained.

"She's always over-tired," said Harry.

"She is only five," said Andy. "Anyway, where are the others?"

"They're just..." Harry peered out of the door.

"Here we are!" Clara's beaming face appeared.

"Great," said Mary. "Well in that case we're off to bed, aren't we Andy? And you two boys had better clear off and give the girls some space now."

"Alright," said Harry amiably.

"Do you girls need a hand sorting out the bed?"

"No, we can do it. Thanks, Mum," said Clara.

They wished each other goodnight then Clara's parents and the boys disappeared into the tiny corridor, pulling the door closed behind them.

"Oh my god, oh my god, oh my god!" Clara said, her cheeks flushed.

"What?" Ada asked, looking for a spider or something equally terrifying.

"He kissed me."

"What?"

"Keep your voice down," Clara hissed. "He kissed me! Gorgeous Daniel!"

47

"No!"

"Yes! Let's get the bed ready and I'll tell you all about it!"

So they pulled the bed into place and got their sleeping bags and pillows, each using the miniscule bathroom once it had been safely vacated by the boys. While Clara was in there, Ada perched on the edge of the bed, feeling excited for her friend but a little bit like a gap had just opened between them. Already there was an age difference of nine months, which didn't always matter but sometimes made itself known. Clara would turn twelve on their second day at secondary school. And now she had moved on a stage in a different way. Still, Ada wanted to know all about it and, once she'd brushed her teeth and used the loo, she wriggled into her sleeping bag next to Clara and said, "Tell me all."

Clara didn't have to be asked twice. She took great delight in every detail; how she had been running to catch up and then Daniel had pulled her hand, and stopped her, under a lamppost, and it was so romantic, and he'd kissed her on the lips, and – "Tongues?" Ada asked, who was not sure what she thought about that kind of kissing – "Urgh, no!" Clara replied, continuing the tale. In the dim light emitted by the kitchen appliances, Ada could see her friend's eyes shining like Georgie's did when she looked at Adam.

And she was pleased for Clara, but a little jealous too, and a tiny bit scared, because what would she do if a boy kissed her? Was she ready for that kind of thing? What if Harry wanted to? Would she let him?

But Harry didn't want to kiss her, because on the second night he paired off with Amelia, a girl his own age who was also staying on the caravan park, and Ada had to hide her disappointment. Clara had to hide her feelings too as it wouldn't do for her parents to discover that she and Daniel liked each other. She told Ada that he was spending time with Harry and Amelia and her friend Esther so that Mary and Andy wouldn't guess what was happening (although as far as Ada could see, nothing was happening).

The days fell into a kind of rhythm, with trips out to the beach or walking on Dartmoor ("Bor-ing!") followed by tea in the caravan and then the youngsters heading down to the entertainment area while Mary and Andy and Lily stayed at the caravan and made the most of the peace and quiet, playing cards on the decking while a warm dusk settled around them.

And then on the last night, Clara's heart was broken for the first time because while Harry was playing pool with Amelia, Daniel took Esther by the hand and led her outside.

"Let's go and see what they're doing," said Clara.

"No, I don't think we should..."

"Come on!" Clara pulled Ada's hand and they went out into the gentle evening air, startling a blackbird which went scooting away, calling out a warning to anyone who would listen.

And of course there they were, Daniel and Esther, tucked behind a corner of the wooden climbing frame and kissing fervently. Ada didn't want to look too closely but she was pretty sure there were tongues.

The journey back was, predictably, not as happy as the journey down, and when they dropped Daniel off at his house, Clara said "Bye then" sarcastically but Ada thought Daniel either didn't notice or just didn't care.

Ada hugged Clara and said a polite thank you to Mary and Andy when it was her turn to be dropped off.

"Bye Ada," said Harry, smiling, but he was back to being Clara's big brother now. Lily hugged her, crying.

"She's going to miss you," said Mary. "You've been great, all that sandcastle-building, and helping her climb those rocks."

"I'll miss you too, Lily," said Ada. And she did. She missed them all.

Louisa, hearing the engine, came out to greet her daughter and say thanks to Clara's parents, and while Ada was so happy to see her, the house seemed very big after the cosy caravan, and life seemed incredibly quiet now it was just her and her mum once more.

Ada

In the morning I wake to a room filled with sunshine, which has soaked through the thin green curtains (summer curtains, Josh has informed me – imagine having different curtains for different seasons!) and I smile as I stretch languorously.

This is the life, I think, and once again Elizabeth Bennett springs to mind. Josh would be mortified if he knew how frequently I am comparing his family life to *Pride and Prejudice* but I can't help it. This is so far removed from my reality it may as well be a Jane Austen novel.

I head down the vast staircase, listening to each creak and looking around me at the severe portraits which adorn the walls – many of which have just been bought at auctions, Josh has informed me, to give the impression of a longer, fuller, family line. Still, the faces that look down seem to judge me, and I suspect they find me wanting. Look at me, in my ripped jeans and t-shirt, my hair scrunched up and fixed with a crocodile clip. The ladies in these paintings are sitting demurely, not a hair out of place but maybe – just maybe – daring a very small, slight smile. The men, meanwhile, look every inch as though they know they belong, that it is only right they should have a spot on the wall of this grand old home, so that future generations (even if they're not of their own family) should look up and revere them. Haughty and serious, these are men in whose presence I would stutter and stammer, and find myself blushing.

But I also know these are paintings done in a particular style, with a very particular purpose in mind. Who knows how accurate they are, and what their subjects were really like? Like the social media of their day, these pictures offered the opportunity to portray a certain image to the world. To record people's likenesses in a particular moment in time. Maybe some of these people were actually very funny, practical jokers, or perhaps they hated the constrictions of society and the expectations placed upon them. They may have been kind philanthropists. Some of them could have been great with children, or animals. These severe-looking portraits tell only one small part of a person's story, and I find that they are creating a spark of an idea within me. I'll keep it to myself for now because, as I've already mentioned, my artistic projects often end in abject disappointment.

Head full of inspiration, I arrive in the hallway and I turn left and right in an attempt to remember which way it is to the dining room. A clatter of cutlery and a burst of laughter remind me, and I push open a highly polished door to find Josh, Rachael, Jack and Sasha sitting at one end of the table, a box of Weetabix and a Kellogg's Variety pack in front of them. There is also an open carton of Aldi orange juice, a teapot, and a bottle of milk.

"Hey, where are the boiled eggs, and your butler?" I ask.

"He said he's not serving you oiks," Josh grins at me. "I've given him the day off; after he dressed me, of course."

"Of course." I give my friend's shoulder a little squeeze and kiss the top of his head before I sit down.

"Sleep OK?" he asks.

"I slept amazingly!" I say.

"No sore head?" asks Sasha, rubbing her own.

"Not for me!" I announce smugly. "But then I only had a couple of glasses. Rather than a couple of bottles."

She groans. "Don't remind me."

"You look very smart though," I say, noting her hair is brushed and shining and set in a low ponytail, and she's wearing some kind of tailored jacket rather than her usual hoodie.

"Yes, Andy and I are off riding this morning."

So it's Andy now? I raise my eyebrows at her.

"Don't look at me like that!" she smiles. "I need to clear my head and a good gallop should blow the cobwebs away."

Is it my imagination, or has Sasha started talking differently, since we've been here? She seems to have stopped dropping her ts, and she's definitely pronouncing things in a more defined way.

***

Andrew had joined us last night for dinner – which was a pile of pizzas plucked from the huge chest freezer – and he was actually a lot less scary than I'd thought. A bit like those portraits, I suppose, maybe he feels he has to present a certain face to the world, particularly when his parents are around. He also made a clear beeline for Sasha and after dinner, while Pippa, Jack and I helped Josh clear things away, the two of them had gone into the library and there was a lot of loud laughter emanating from that room.

After the work was done, Archie and Rachael reappeared – "Very convenient," Josh said, grinning.

"We'll do our stint tomorrow," Archie promised.

"Sure. I spent three years living with you, remember? I know your track record."

"Ah but I made up for it with my sparkling company and ready wit." Archie put a friendly arm around Josh's shoulders and smiled at me. I looked away, suddenly a little bit shy, hoping the others wouldn't notice.

"If you say so." Josh leaned his head briefly on Archie's shoulder. "Anyway, come on, let's go and have some fun."

With Will and Charlotte busy elsewhere, six of us went into the extensive living room and Josh opened a great trunk full of board games. Archie discovered a Bluetooth speaker on a shelf and paired it to his phone so we could all listen to his choice of music – again – and in time Andrew and Sasha joined us. We played cards, and Monopoly, and by the time we had finished there were more than a few empty wine bottles on the table. Archie and Jack had nipped off at regular intervals, coming back smelling of weed, and when Andrew had cottoned on to this he'd gone out to join them, and Sasha had decided to tag along.

I'm not a big drinker and I knew I didn't want a hangover while we were here so I'd switched to water early on, but even so the atmosphere in the room had me feeling like I was drunk anyway. Archie turned the volume up and then Josh protested that all we'd heard was Archie's tunes so we took it in turns to choose the music and started to compile a playlist that we agreed we'd share, to remind us of this weekend. It didn't get dark until very late, and around half past ten we all went outside to see the bats dancing against the backdrop of the darkening sky. Solar lights twinkled along the length of the red-brick garden walls and the air was filled with the scent from Antonia's rose garden.

"Mum loves her roses," Andrew said, taking a pen knife from his pocket and neatly clipping a flower to hand to Sasha.

"I thought it was Mummy," I found myself saying, before I'd had a chance to think about it. I immediately reddened, though hopefully it was too dark for anyone else to notice. I did see Archie turn his head and grin at me. Thankfully Andrew just laughed.

"Mummy to her face," he said. "Honestly, I don't know why she likes it so much but if it keeps her happy..."

"You're very good at that," said Josh.

"Hey, it's my job, little brother. I don't have the freedom you do."

"True. But you do get the house."

"Also true!"

They laughed, and I liked their easiness. I can imagine it could be a situation fraught with jealousy and envy; the older brother gets it all.

"At least you don't have to take a position as a vicar, Josh," I'd said, again speaking before thinking.

"What?" Archie had spluttered.

"It's what used to happen," I'd protested. "The older brother would take on the house and the position in society and the younger one would have to go into a respectable position like being a vicar."

"My god, she's back on *Pride and Prejudice*," Josh had groaned.

"I do see myself as a Mr Darcy," Andrew had mused.

"I can see that," said Sasha, and Josh had nudged me.

We sat out on the grass, which was becoming cool in the evening air, and I listened as the birds called to each other, the blackbirds relaying their urgent last-minute messages before settling down for the night. While the sky grew so dark that we could no longer see the bats, I heard a pheasant exclaiming indignantly in a nearby field. An owl called, and then another. I felt a hand on my back and I realised it was Archie's. He stroked my hair, inviting me to lean against him, and I did, closing my eyes for just a moment. If anyone else noticed, nobody said anything, and I let myself relax, watching the stars shyly reveal themselves and the thin layer of cloud cover move rapidly before the waxing moon. The owls called again and there was movement near the garden wall, setting off a security light. I turned and saw the figure of a fox, stopped dead-still in the light.

"Look!" I said, and Josh turned towards me. I saw him rapidly take in Archie's arm around me. I sat up straight. "A fox," I said, pointing.

It turned its head towards us and in my mind our eyes met, but I know that couldn't have been. It was just aware of us suddenly and it took a moment to assess whether we were any threat. I was gratified to see it trot off into the shadows. We had not scared it.

"Right, I'm going in," said Josh.

"I'm coming with you," I said.

"You don't have to."

"No, I'm tired, and I'm starting to feel cold."

"OK," said Josh, and he stood and pulled me up. I linked my arm through his and was pleased when he squeezed my hand. "Hot chocolate?" he asked.

"That would be perfect."

We left the others outside and headed to the kitchen, where I stood warming myself by the Aga while Josh got out the oat milk and a tub of cocoa.

"This is going to be very dark," he warned, "I'll put in some sugar."

"Lovely," I smiled.

"Ada?"

"Yes?"

"You and Archie…"

I spluttered. "There is no me and Archie! We're just mates. Anyway, he wouldn't be interested in me…"

"Oh god, don't do that, please."

"Do what?"

"Say 'he wouldn't be interested in me'. As though he's some sex god and you're not worthy."

"That's not what I'm doing."

"Isn't it? Anyway, it's none of my business, but…"

"You're right, it's not," I had huffed, but I'd seen his shoulders stiffen as he'd turned to whisk the cocoa into the milk.

I softened and moved behind him, putting my arms around his waist. "Honestly, Josh, there is no me and Archie, and I don't think he's a sex god or that I'm not worthy. I just mean, well we're friends, aren't we? Like you and me. Well not quite like you and me because you and me are best friends, aren't we?" I laid my head against the back of his shoulder, my eyes feeling sore and tired.

"We are," he'd said, and I'd felt him relax. He turned and put his arms around me. "Always and forever."

"I hope so."

"I know so. And look, it really is none of my business, if you and Archie... I just..."

"Ssh," I'd said. "Not going to happen."

And we'd hugged for a few moments more then Josh had switched to business-like mode, heating up the cocoa until it was steaming, then pouring it into chunky blue mugs. "Here," he'd said. "Take this to bed with you, it'll give you sweet dreams."

"Thank you, Josh." I'd kissed him on the cheek.

We walked up the stairs together and went our separate ways – he to the west and me to the east. I went to the open window and took a moment to let the soft breeze whisper in and gently touch the skin of my face. I closed my eyes. I could hear laughter and shouts from outside and I smiled at the sound of my friends out there. Then I pulled the window nearly fully shut and closed the curtains, pulled off my jeans and climbed gratefully into bed. Sitting up against the ridiculously comfortable pillows, I sipped my drink. It was rich and sweet and just the right temperature and I took my time to savour it, looking around my room and wondering about the people who had slept here before me.

Imagining what ghosts might haunt this house, I'd switched off my light, too tired to go and brush my teeth, and I'd slipped into a deep, easy sleep.

***

This morning, while Sasha and Andrew take themselves off riding, Josh offers to give me a tour of the different gardens and outbuildings. "Then we could set up some outside games, maybe have a picnic by the lake..."

"That sounds absolutely magical," I say. I haven't yet seen Archie but that's not unusual. He'll have been up late and might not surface until after lunch.

"Seems like Andrew and Sasha have hit it off," I say.

"Yes, well, that one's been on the cards for a while."

"Really?"

"Yes, you know our families know each other; not hugely well, but we mix in the same circles."

Even that phrase seems so alien to me. I imagine balls and society functions, Christmas parties at each other's mansions, and I smile as I picture Sasha as a debutante, being introduced into society.

"Sasha seems different here," I say.

"Yes, I suppose she does. I think she's just good at fitting in. She flits between different worlds, and gets on with everyone."

"You're absolutely right. She does just seem to know how to talk to anyone, whatever their age or background."

"She'd be good for Andrew."

"So you wouldn't mind then, if the two of them get together?"

"No, why would I? At least I'd know I like this girlfriend. He's had some shockers!"

"Really?"

"Really."

I want to ask Josh now, about himself, but I can't quite bring myself to. He will tell me when he's ready, if he is ready, if there is anything to tell.

Instead I ask him about what it was like growing up here, and going to boarding school.

"I know I was so lucky in so many ways but honestly, it's quite isolating. And there were times when I was away when I just wished I could come home after school. There wasn't much downtime, or privacy. You know I like my time to myself. There wasn't much of that at school. Maybe that's the reason I like it now. But it wasn't all bad, not at all. We're all a product of our experiences anyway, aren't we? And I developed my love of art at school, and got to go on trips to Florence and Rome and New York, so yes, I was very lucky."

I watch him while he's speaking; his long, dark lashes and his unkempt dark hair. He's not a lot taller than me, and he's got quite a slight frame, unlike his bigger, rugby-playing brother. I feel a rush of love for my friend.

"You're a good person, Josh."

"You're not so bad yourself," he smiles at me.

"We're both pretty awesome actually," I observe.

"Now we have to find ways to carry on being awesome."

"I know. I know. I fear for my future, Josh, I really do."

We are approaching a bench, in a little nook of the walled garden, and without either of us suggesting it, we both sit. I watch a bee burrow into a large purple flower.

"Why?"

"Well, I don't know. What can I really do with my degree? And could I ever make it as an artist? Who really does that? I mean really?"

"Tracey Emin. Grayson Perry."

"Don't say Banksy."

"Why not? He found his own way to do it. Some people do. Why not you?"

"Or you?" I suggest.

He smiles. "I don't know. Maybe my family will put pressure on me to become a vicar."

"Sorry about that," I grin, abashed. "I think I've got a bit carried away with myself. I tell you what, though, I've had a bit of inspiration while I've been here…"

"Oh yeah?"

"Yes. I'm still thinking it through though." I don't like to give anything away but those portraits are still swirling through my mind.

"Whatever you do, Ada, make it amazing. OK?"

"I'll try."

We sit companionably for a while, and then there's a shout from along the path. It's Archie, I see, and my heart rate increases.

"Budge up!" he says, nudging me along the seat. I oblige, and I'm squashed between the two of them.

"Alright?" Josh asks good-naturedly and although I'm glad to see Archie, I'm sorry that my moment of peace with my friend has been broken.

2013

Soon enough, the summer was nearly over and it was time for making sure they had the right uniform and PE kits, and school bags, and shoes which fitted them comfortably. Shorts and t-shirts were put away until next year, assuming they hadn't grown out of them by then.

Mary gave Clara and Ada a lift on their first day at secondary school. The girls sat in the back and Harry in the passenger seat. He practically leaped out of the car as soon as they pulled up, and they saw him run up to Daniel.

"Never mind him," said Ada.

"I don't. I'm over boys. It's friends first with me, always."

"Same," Ada said happily.

Reluctantly, they unclipped their seatbelts. Mary turned and smiled at them. "Good luck, girls. You'll be fine!"

"Mum, are you crying?" asked Clara.

Ada noticed that Mary's eyes did look a bit shiny.

"Only a bit! You're just… so grown up."

"Mum!" Clara said in disgust, and that was enough to have her following her brother's lead and also exiting the car swiftly.

"Thank you Mary," said Ada, who sometimes wished that her own mum was a bit more like Clara's.

This morning, Louisa had left at her usual time. She had given Ada an extra tight hug, going on to hold her at length and examine her.

"What?" Ada had asked, laughing.

"Just checking you're OK."

"What would you do if I wasn't?"

"I… don't know!" Louisa had laughed, and pulled a ten-pound note from her pocket. "Put this somewhere safe and treat yourself and Clara to a milkshake on your way home, if that's alright with Mary."

"Thanks Mum!"

"My pleasure. Now go and knock them dead!"

And Louisa had gone to work, leaving Ada alone in an empty house. She had been adamant that she no longer needed a childminder and so Grace had been given three months' notice but Louisa told her she didn't have to work those months. Grace had been more than happy with that, and was currently in a Greek hotel sleeping off a hangover, blissfully unaware that her former charge was about to embark on a whole new, scary adventure.

Ada had turned the radio up loud so the house didn't seem so echoey, and she brushed her teeth, fastened her hair into a ponytail, and checked then re-checked she had everything she needed in her bag.

Now, for a fleeting moment, she found she wanted to hang on to Mary, to say perhaps there had been a mistake and actually she still had one more year at that friendly, familiar primary school where she had first met Clara. But her friend was waiting for her.

Ada exited the car and the two girls walked side by side towards the enormous hulk of a school that loomed before them.

Ada

The weather is incredibly kind to us this weekend and we gather in the kitchen at lunchtime while Josh and Andrew pull various items out of the fridge – all from Waitrose but nevertheless it's a bit different to what I'd expected. I think of last night's pizzas, and this morning's boxes of cereal and Aldi orange juice. I'd assumed Josh's family would have a housekeeper or a cook at the very least.

"We get people in if we're having a function," Andrew says, "but otherwise we fend for ourselves."

While I don't especially want to make the observation that pre-prepared salads, quiches and Scotch eggs from Waitrose are not exactly reflective of having to fend for themselves, I realise it's not really that different to my home life with Mum. She has always been too busy to cook and she and I have relied extensively on M&S, Waitrose and Sainsbury's. I do enjoy cooking and I always liked visiting Gran and making food with her – she even makes her bread from scratch. Josh has also inspired me and shown me that it's possible to make all sorts of things that we might otherwise buy ready-made – cakes, pastry, pasta, tortilla wraps. We have been trying to perfect crumpets but that is proving a step too far at the moment. It seems like Josh hides this side of himself when he's at home and I wonder why.

Today he is more than happy to just bring on the Waitrose picnic, and it turns out he and Andrew had compiled a shopping list together over the last week or two, and Andrew took delivery of it all yesterday, which is actually quite sweet. With their parents out of the way, Josh's big brother seems to have softened a little and I can perhaps see a little bit more of why Sasha might like him. The pair of them pluck bottles of champagne from the wine fridge and Andrew fills buckets with ice. They take them outside then return for glasses. The rest of us take out platters of sandwiches and tubs of salads, punnets of strawberries, and bags of posh crisps.

We lay out the blankets on the grass, once more looking out over the horses' field and across the flat landscape. The trees are at their finest, in full leaf and bursting with the joys of late spring. The weather has not yet been consistently hot enough to dry out the grass, so everywhere we turn is green.

Tucking into the food, the others chat away but I just want to sit and take it all in. The scenery; the freshness of the air; the birdsong and occasional panicked outcry of pheasants; my friends' voices and laughter, all so familiar after three years together. I wonder when we will all be together again and as I finish my first glass of champagne, the bubbles go to my head and I find I'm a little melancholy at the thought. Where yesterday I had been buoyed up at the world opening before me, I now feel like stepping out into it also means that there is a door closing behind me.

"Alright?" Josh asks, nudging me.

"Yes, I think so. I mean, yes. This is lovely, Josh. This… everything…" I swing my arm expansively.

He smiles. "I'm glad. I'm so glad you're here. I'm so glad we met."

We click glasses and, seeing mine is empty, he fills it up. I don't stop him.

"I'm going to miss you," I say.

"I'm going to miss you," he replies. "Maybe I'll move to Cornwall."

"I don't know if I'm going to stay there," I say.

"You would if I moved down!"

"Maybe." I smile. "I don't know what to do, really. Where I'm going to live."

"You're going to your mum's after this weekend though?"

"Yes, of course. But I… it's a bit weird, with her and Jude."

My mum is in a relatively new relationship, and it's with a woman – something else which is new, or news to me at least. And I don't have a problem with it, I really don't. Jude is great and Mum is so happy. But she lives in a flat, and while Jude has her own place, they do spend most of their time together, at Mum's. They would never in a million years think that I was in the way if I moved in, and would hate it if they thought I felt that way. But I've had my own space for a while now and even back in London, before uni, Mum was out so much, usually working, that I had a lot of time to myself. I worry that living in Mum's flat might make me feel a bit trapped. There are balconies but no other outside space, and it's right by the harbour, which is great for a holiday, but would I actually want to live there?

And, love Cornwall as I do, what would I do there? I am more than aware from Mum and Jude, who both work at the food bank – well, Jude runs it and Mum volunteers there – that it's a tough place to earn a living. Great if you're already set up; if you've already made your fortune, like Mum has, but I am just starting out.

With no familiar home to return to, I'm all at sea, which is quite fitting really, but not especially helpful. So I suppose that's why I'm feeling a little bit down as well; my uni days are over, my friends are all going their separate ways, and I don't really have any roots anymore.

I will go back to Mum's for the summer and try to get some seasonal work while I figure out my next steps. Mum thinks I might be able to get some lifeguard work at one of the local beaches, as I'm qualified and I've had some hours while I've been at uni, but I suspect those positions will have been filled long ago.

"Well, I'm coming to visit next month," Josh says. "I'll try and borrow Mum's car and we can be holiday-makers. Art tourists. We'll make a plan. OK?"

"OK."

I smile at him, feeling a little bit better and sure that, even if the others move on and our friendship group dissipates, I will always have Josh.

"I'm not going anywhere without you," he says.

"Steady on." I smile, but I'm pleased. I lean against him, grateful for his steady, solid support.

After an hour or two, there are empty plastic containers piled haphazardly next to one of the stone lions and a number of empty champagne bottles discarded on the grass. We have switched down a gear to prosecco, and

I'm taking a break from alcohol, sipping a cold ginger beer. The sun is high above us, throwing its heat down liberally. Will is lying on his back, resting his head on Charlotte's leg while she strokes his hair. Rachael and Jack have disappeared off 'for a walk', to knowing smiles between the rest of us.

"I want to swim!" Sasha announces.

"Yes!" says Archie.

"Erm…" Josh says. "Not in the lake."

"Why not?" Sasha asks.

"It's not really a swimming lake. It's full of weed, and the swans are nesting, and…"

"It'll be fine," Andrew says, standing up.

"Andy…" Josh says.

"Course it will. People have been swimming there for years."

"Yeah, but we've all been drinking too."

"It'll sober us up. Then we can have a snooze before beginning all over again."

"Yes!" says Sasha.

"Have you even got stuff for swimming in?" Josh asks.

"We've got our underwear," Archie says. "Assuming we're all wearing any. Who's up for it? Ada?"

I look at Josh. "No, I'm alright," I say. I'd actually love a swim, but I don't want to upset Josh.

Archie shrugs. "Pippa? Charlotte? Will?"

Will just slowly shakes his head, his eyes still closed and a small smile on his lips. "I am quite fine here, thank you." Charlotte shrugs and shakes her head as well.

"Looks like it's just us then," Archie says to Andrew and Sasha. I'm pretty sure they'd prefer it if it was just the two of them but he seems not to have noticed.

The three of them head off together, disappearing round the side of the house, laughing and pushing each other. I can tell Josh is annoyed.

"Come on," I say, "shall we get the giant Jenga? Pippa, want to play?" I think she might feel a little bit left out now that Sasha has latched on to Andrew.

"Yes! That sounds great."

"Come on then. Tell you what, let's clear up the lunch stuff as well, shall we?"

"Sure, just give me a mo," says Pippa, lying down and clearly having no intention of getting up to help.

Josh goes to get up but I put a hand on his shoulder. "You just stay and chill," I say. "Honestly, you've done loads to organise this weekend. I'll just take a couple of empty bottles to the recycling and bring back the Jenga."

"Should I make some tea, though? Coffee, maybe? Liven everyone up a bit?" He looks meaningfully at Pippa, and Will.

"Lazy blighters, the lot of us!" laughs Charlotte. "I'll bring some stuff in soon, I promise. So will Will, won't you?" She nudges him with her leg.

"Ow! Yeah, sure. Course I will."

"Leave the coffee," I say to Josh. "Just relax for a bit. We'll play a few games and maybe when the others are back from their swim we can get some hot drinks then."

"Alright," Josh says and he doesn't protest anymore. Instead, he sinks back onto the blanket, alongside Pippa. "Maybe I'll just rest my eyes for a few minutes."

"Good idea," says Charlotte and Will moves so that she can lie alongside him, laying her arm across his stomach.

I look down at the four of them and I smile, fairly sure they'll all be asleep in minutes.

I drag over a sun umbrella and stand and put it over them.

"Who stole the sun?" mumbles Josh.

"Just protecting you all," I say. "You know, just in the unlikely event of you dozing off."

"Thanks Mum," grins Will.

"Watch it," I smile and pick up a couple of the empty bottles then walk across the gravel and through the open doorway into the dark, echoing hallway of the house.

A couple of flies buzz frustratedly at the windows, desperately trying to get into the light. I try to let them out and see the curled-up bodies of those who have gone before them and failed in their attempts. The windows won't budge so I have to leave the insects to their fate.

My eyes travel across the paintings again and up along the portraits which adorn the stairwell. There are men, women, children, horses, dogs. All long since gone from this world. I hear a creaking from somewhere upstairs and for a moment I think I can hear footsteps. This place is so old, it almost seems crazy to think that it might not be haunted.

I shake the thought away. I don't mind the idea of ghosts but in a house of this age and size, it feels like the walls hold so many echoes of the past, keeping secrets safe and concealing misdemeanours of its past occupants, as people have lived or tried to live up to the expectations of society, and fit themselves into the roles which have been carved out for them. They may have been lacking for nothing materially but would that have made them happy? Mrs Bennett and her girls spring to mind once more, pressed into their neat little moulds, spending afternoons sewing and embroidering; reading or playing the piano. *All young ladies are accomplished,* I think, paraphrasing the lovely Mr Bingham. Andrew might fancy himself as Mr Darcy but I'd put Josh as Bingham, though I am not sure he'd thank me for it.

I study the female portraits. The solemn, composed expressions. How boring it must have been to be a woman in society. Sitting up straight and keeping their figures. Just waiting to receive visitors. Did they feel ensnared, confined by the restrictions of society and their position within it, or did they believe that life was exactly as it should be? And what about the people who worked here? The servants. Did they believe that their rightful place was to wait upon these other humans?

We've talked a lot in our late-night student discussions about the way some people have of deferring to their 'betters', how some people believe that they are actually better, more entitled, than others.

Archie believes it is an effect of having a royal family. "Why on earth do people bow down before them like they're better than any one of us?"

He thinks we should have thrown over the aristocracy, like they did in France. Some of the others looked slightly uncomfortable at this idea.

Could this house have trapped any resilient, rebellious spirits who wanted to live life differently but could never escape? I can't help but shiver a little at the thought.

I look over my shoulder then cast a glance at the portraits again, imagining once more what these people might make of me. I imagine them looking at me with distaste, even mocking me, sniggers hidden behind manicured, lily-white hands. I hurry through to the kitchen and for a moment I think I can hear laughter behind me, ringing around the empty hall.

Recycling safely stowed away, I head out of the back door – the servants' door in days gone by – feeling like I am in a more comfortable place. I walk across the patio and look down the slope, seeing at first just an empty lake at the bottom and then recognising Archie, though I can see no sign of Andrew or Sasha.

"Hi!" I shout, but receive no response. He's got his back to me, so maybe he can't hear me. I call out once more and he looks around, taking a moment to locate me.

"Ada!" he yells, and I think how romantic this could be, the two of us calling to each other; imagine living here with him, we could… I realise that he's waving at me, and shouting something else. "Help!" I take a moment to check I heard right and then I hear it again. "Ada! Help!"

Without a second thought, I'm racing down the slope towards the lake.

"I'm coming Archie, just hang on!" I shout, ripping off my shoes and diving in. With the shock of the cold water on this hot day comes the memory of Josh's words: "It's not really a swimming lake. It's full of weed…"

Too late now. I'm already in, and Archie is out there in the middle of the water. It won't take long to get to him, though I'd be faster in my swimsuit.

"Hang on!" I shout again and begin to thrash, front crawl, towards him, pushing my own fears out of my mind. This is what I've been trained for, though I've never yet had to put my skills into any action more dangerous than reuniting a child with her mother or shouting at swimmers to go between the red-and-yellow

72

flags. I had a megaphone then and I wish I had one now, so that I could call the others. Where are Sasha and Andrew, anyway?

In just moments, out of breath, I reach Archie. My muscles are painfully alive with the sudden exertion. "Archie!" I gasp. "Are you OK?"

He turns to me, and he grins. "I'm fine," he says. "I just wanted to get you in here with me."

"You idiot!" I splutter, but the relief pours through me and I begin to laugh, then Archie puts his arm around my waist and pulls me to him.

"I'm sorry you got your clothes wet on my behalf," he says.

"I was worried, you dickhead."

"I'm sorry. I really am." I see his lashes are wet and long, clinging together. And he's looking into my eyes, and his sun-kissed face, speckled with tiny water particles sparkling in the light, is moving towards me, and his lips are nearly touching mine, and...

"What the fuck is going on?" I hear from behind me, and I turn to see Josh in a rowing boat, which now drifts towards us. I turn and put my hand out to steady it and stop it from running into us.

"It's Archie," I say. "I thought he was in trouble."

"It's my fault," Archie admits. "I thought it would be funny. I know Ada's an amazing swimmer and a lifeguard, and I thought I'd see what she'd do if she thought I was drowning."

"For fuck's sake, Archie, I told you this isn't a swimming lake. You risked your own safety, and Ada's."

"Sorry mate," Archie says, but his hand is still on my waist, and he gives me a playful squeeze.

73

I'm aware suddenly how heavy my clothes feel and I can see Josh was really worried.

"Sorry, Josh," I say.

"You've got nothing to be sorry for, Ada. Come on, I'll pull you in and row you back to shore."

Josh holds his hand out and I take it, reluctantly letting Archie's hand slither down my thigh.

Once I'm in I turn back but Josh is already rowing away.

"What about Archie?" I ask.

"He can make his own way back," Josh says grimly. "Were you two kissing?" he asks, accusingly.

"No, we… of course not. I'd only just got to him when you shouted to us. Only just realised he was kidding."

"It was really stupid," Josh says, his mouth a thin line.

"You're right," I say, "it was." But I can't help watching Archie as he swims across to the closest edge of the lake to him, pushing himself out with those strong arms and revealing a muscular, tanned back above his black shorts. "Sorry Josh," I say again.

"I told you," Josh says, "you don't have anything to be sorry for."

But it feels like he's annoyed at me as much as he is at Archie. By the time we're tying the boat up, I can tell he's trying to be himself again, but this incident has got to him. I go to give him a hug but he holds me at arm's length. "You're covered in weed," he manages to smile. "Go and get a shower and get changed. I'll put those things through the wash for you."

I do as I'm told, stripping off my outer layers in the boot room so I don't drip too much smelly water and weed through the house. A walk of shame below the judgy portraits and I realise I may not have imagined the creaking or the laughter earlier. I recognise Sasha's voice, and Andrew's, from along the family corridor, and realise why Archie was alone in the lake. Well at least the weekend is going well for some of us.

After my shower, and in a fresh set of clothes, I wander back down the stairs and outside to find the others. Will and Charlotte are still asleep on a blanket in the shade, sweetly oblivious to all that's gone on, while Jack and Rachael have returned and are playing Jenga with Josh and Pippa. There is no sign of Archie and I go to lie on a blanket by myself, letting my hair dry in the sun and listening to the sweet birdsong. I'm suddenly exhausted and, even with the turmoil of thoughts of the almost-kiss and a slight niggling at the back of my mind that Josh is not happy, I find my eyes closing. I drift off into a strange, half-awake state, where I catch myself falling asleep and try to prevent it, only to fall back again, odd and confusing dreams scudding through my mind like clouds across the sky.

2014

By the end of year seven, Ada no longer felt like she wanted to be back at primary school; although she still thought fondly of the place, it all seemed so babyish, and when the current year sixes had come up for move-up day they'd seemed so little, and fresh. Green.

Not that it had been an easy year. Definitely a baptism by fire. Ada and Clara were both easy girls to get on with and thankfully had each other, but they'd not gone entirely unscathed. The older kids thought it their right to yank off the stupid clip-on ties which formed part of the new school uniform; as if to reiterate the youthfulness of the year sevens, the new headteacher had decided to make her mark by updating everything – but reasonably had decided the older years should not need to buy the smarter, more expensive items like blazers and ties and very specific skirts. This meant that the incoming youngest children stood out like sore thumbs. The ties were a novelty in themselves and provided much amusement for those in the higher years.

In addition to the tie-pulling, there had been an incident where a year nine boy had sent the girls completely the wrong way when they had a technology lesson, and they'd arrived ten minutes late and red-faced. They were sure he'd done it on purpose, but what could they do?

All of this on top of becoming familiar with adhering to a timetable, learning the layout of the school, dealing with teachers who could be fantastic fun one day and ferocious the next. But soon they would no longer be the youngest in the school, and Ada had recently passed the milestone of turning twelve – while Clara was rushing headlong towards being a teenager. And on top of all this, they had ten whole days together in Cornwall to look forward to. Life was looking up.

Mary laughed when Louisa opened the boot, seeing that both girls had managed to fill three bags each of clothes, books, games, and electronic devices.

"The weather's changeable in Cornwall," Ada had protested when Louisa questioned the need for quite so much luggage. "You're always saying that. So we're bringing enough things for every kind of weather."

"Alright, alright," Louisa caved in. It really didn't matter, though she wasn't sure where they'd find the space to store all of this in her mum's little house. Luckily she had booked into a hotel so at least the girls could have a bedroom each.

And as it turned out, the weather was glorious. Clara, who had never been to Cornwall before, was beguiled by the long stretches of white-sanded beaches, and the harbour, and the surfers.

"I'm going to learn to do that," she said to Ada, watching a wetsuited woman seemingly effortlessly riding a wave back in to shore.

"Me too. Let's ask Mum if we can have lessons."

And Louisa, feeling unusually relaxed and at ease with herself, willingly agreed. She had the best of both worlds during this holiday; it was a chance to see her mum and spend time with her, but she also had the space and luxury of the hotel when she needed time to herself. The girls had each other so Louisa didn't feel the need to entertain them and they were old enough now to be trusted to go off by themselves as long as they kept her informed of their plans, and stayed in close contact. It was good for them to have some independence, she told herself; good for her mum to have some company, and good for her relationship with her mum that they weren't on top of each other.

There were times she felt something that she couldn't quite define, like when she arrived at Godolphin Terrace to find Elise and the girls baking in the kitchen. Louisa herself had been on her laptop for nearly three hours, and when she saw this domestic scene and heard the laughter when Clara accidentally tipped a sieve-full of flour across the work surface, it wasn't that she was jealous as such – nor did she feel guilty – but she did have this vague sense that she was missing out on something. Was it time with her mum, or time with her daughter? Or just the simple things which came with a more ordinary life that wasn't ruled by work? Or, she wondered, was she feeling guilty that she never took the time to do things like baking with Ada, when she knew full well how much she'd loved doing that with Elise when she'd been younger?

Ah well, Ada benefitted in other ways, and Louisa was always telling Elise that she should come to London for a visit (though if she was very honest, she knew that this was unlikely, and she wondered what she would do if her mum ever accepted such an invitation).

Elise, meanwhile, was delighted to have the girls in her house, and to be busy and needed again. She showed them her attic and let them use some of her paints and canvases. In truth, she was really becoming a bit beyond getting up to her much-loved space in the roof these days and she knew that in the winter the cold and the inevitable damp in the air from being so close to the sea would be enough to put her off entirely. The girls loved the room though, and Elise could see how proud Ada was, showing her friend the view from the window and the seagulls' nest on the roof of the extension next door.

In the afternoons, while Elise had a nap – "Call it a siesta, Gran!" – the girls would go to the beach or wander along the harbourside, spending their coins in the amusement arcade or watching the boys go by.

"Friends first, though!" Ada would remind Clara.

"Always."

They would link arms and walk together, pretending not to notice any admiring glances from the local boys who were messing around with their skateboards, although Clara couldn't resist a quick glance back when she thought Ada wasn't looking.

And in the evening, they'd eat out, all four of them. Elise had offered to cook, more than once, but Louisa had insisted on taking them out – "My treat" – and they'd had Chinese, and Indian, and expensive seafood; stone-baked pizza; fish and chips in the garden of a lovely old pub...

"I've never eaten so much in my life," Elise had said, patting her full belly. "Not that I'm complaining," she'd added quickly, eager to make sure she did not upset her daughter.

When the girls were asleep, Elise couldn't resist looking in on Ada, just watching her from the doorway, sleeping peacefully, her mouth puckered open. She still was such a child, though she was undeniably growing up.

But asleep, Ada was unguarded and innocent, and her youth shone through. It brought to mind a night a long time ago when Elise had left Louisa in bed, and Laurie; locked them both in their rooms...

She shook her head, pressed that memory and all its accompanying feelings back into the little box she kept in the furthest, darkest corner of her mind. That was not for now, she told herself. That was not for any time, ever.

Ada

"Ada!" There is quite a welcoming party for me when I step off the train. Mum, Gran, Jude and Stevie, the teenage daughter of Gran's friend Maggie.

"Hello!" I laugh. "I wasn't expecting all this."

I step into an embrace from my mum, and it feels good. Really good.

By the time I left Josh's house this morning, that nagging feeling that I had upset him had only got worse.

"Have I done something?" I asked him, while he lay on the sofa in my room, watching me pack.

"No!" he'd exclaimed. "You really haven't. It's just me. And the thought of everything being over. Perhaps I've caught what you had yesterday."

"It's not over," I had tried to console him, despite the fact I was still feeling like that. Only now I had this little glimmer of hope about Archie. I knew it wasn't the right thing to mention to Josh, though. I could hardly expect him to feel happy about that. "It's just beginning. You said yourself, you'll be coming to visit me in Cornwall soon. And we can start to make some plans."

"I guess I don't want to be stuck here either," he said and, as he heard the words escape his mouth, he recognised how ridiculous they sounded. "I mean, look at this place. It's only got twelve bedrooms and three hundred acres."

"You're right, it's a dump. Imagine being stuck here."

I threw a cushion at him, and he lobbed it back at me.

"Ow!" I said. "Don't take it out on me, just because you've got to stay in a hovel."

"It's awful isn't it? I'm such a spoiled brat. But I'm going to miss you, Ada. And everyone. Well not Sasha, as she's staying here with my dear brother."

I had raised my eyebrows at this. "What do you think your mum and dad will say?"

"Oh, they'll love it! Sasha's perfect daughter-in-law material."

"Bloody hell, it's a bit early for that, isn't it?"

"You'd think. But in this world, things get decided pretty quickly. Still, I know Sasha's got a mind of her own. Andy, too. But they do seem to be getting on well."

"Time will tell, I suppose."

"What about you and Archie?" Josh had asked then, not looking at me.

"Me and Archie?" I said, as though the thought had never entered my mind, but Josh can always see right through me.

"Come on!"

"Well, nothing will come of that, I don't suppose. I'm not sure there's anything there anyway. He was just messing about yesterday."

"He was a twat yesterday."

"Yes, he was. He'll go on and do whatever it is he wants to do. Become the next Banksy or something…"

"Or be mightily disappointed and end up working in a boring office."

"That is also a possibility. For all of us, I hate to say. Well, maybe not you."

"Why not me?"

"Because you're on course to join the Church, remember?"

"Oh yes. The Second Son. Thanks for reminding me."

Jack was driving Charlotte, Will, Rachael and Pippa over to London, where they would all disperse and go their separate ways, so Josh gave me and Archie a lift to the station. It was a slightly awkward car journey, with Archie in the back and me sitting in the passenger seat trying to make conversation that would include all three of us. It's not that Josh wasn't talking to Archie but he was clearly still pissed off with him. And the previous evening had been a lot more subdued than the first night, with Jack and Archie driving to the nearest town (half an hour away) to pick up a curry for everyone. When they'd returned, we'd sat around chatting and eating, but one by one (or in some cases two by two) had drifted off to bed early. I'd gone up to my own room feeling deflated but unable to shake the memory of the glistening, tanned skin of Archie's face as his mouth had approached mine.

In the car on the way to the station I had to pretend that I wasn't in any way affected by what had happened – or nearly happened – in the lake and I was also wondering what we would do when we got to the station. My train was due to leave ten minutes before Archie's. Would he wait with me on the platform? Kiss me goodbye? Stand waving at me through clouds of steam as my train drew away... OK, I was getting a bit carried away there.

What actually happened was that Josh got out of the car and helped us get our bags from the boot. He hugged me, and shook Archie's hand, and I promised to message him when I got to Cornwall safely. Then he got back in his car and drove away and I felt something deep within, like the twisting of a key in a lock, at the sight of him going. I've been so used to seeing Josh almost every single day these last three years – often multiple times a day. He's my best friend, as well as Clara, and my safety net. What was I going to do without him?

I turned to Archie, chin up. "Shall we go in?"

"After you," he said, all gentleman-like, though he didn't go as far as to offer to help me with my bags. Not that I wanted him to.

We got to the ticket gates and once we were through the other side, examined the departure screens.

"Looks like you're that way and I'm this way," said Archie.

"Looks like it," I agreed.

"So, I guess it's bye for now."

"I guess so," I said, interested in the 'for now'.

"I can't believe we've finished uni," Archie said, and it felt like he was buying some time.

"I know. Weird, isn't it?"

"So weird. Onwards and upwards, eh?"

"I guess." I felt like crying and I only hoped it wasn't written all over my face.

"I see great things ahead for you, Ada. Stay true to yourself, won't you? I know that sounds cheesy."

I'd smiled. "Cheesy, but nice."

"Honestly, you're a gem and you don't even know it."

Was he going to kiss me? Would this be the moment

that it finally happened? He reached for me, but just swept me up in a huge hug. "Love you, mate."

Mate? *Mate?* Is there a worse word in the whole of the English dictionary? Never mind the 'love you' bit; that meant nothing. The 'mate' was like a pin in the side of a balloon. All my hopes burst that second. But then...

"Can I come and see you? In Cornwall?"

"Yes. Yes, of course. I mean, I'll have to check with Mum, but I'm sure that will be fine."

"Great. I'll be in touch."

And he was gone, lugging his rucksack on his back, vanishing off up the stairs to the bridge across the tracks, and I was left alone.

Now though, I am far from alone, and everyone wants to ask me questions, or so it would seem.

"How was your journey?" (Jude)

"Are you hungry?" (Gran)

"Did you have a big party at Josh's mansion?" (Stevie)

"How's Josh?" (Mum)

"One at a time!" I'd laughed. Jude has taken my bag from me, and Mum has linked her arm through mine as we make our merry way to the car. It's a glorious sunny, blue-skied day in Cornwall and I'm suddenly so happy to be here. After the slightly cool morning at Josh's, and the sadness of leaving uni life behind, I feel wrapped up in the warmth of my family, not to mention the heat of the sun, which soaks into my muscles while the sound of the gulls overhead and the sea so close by fill me with an unexpected joy. Memories of summers past flood into me, of arriving here with Mum, then as I got a little bit older venturing a couple of train journeys alone (with the train guard primed to keep an eye on me, and Gran ready and waiting for me half an hour before my train was due in) or with Clara, coming to stay with Gran and enjoy the local night life (and meet the local boys). It may not be home, but it is so familiar and now that I'm here I don't feel as out of place as I'd thought I might.

I guess the transitions between places and different parts of life are always going to be difficult. Stepping into the unknown and leaving something not only known but loved behind. But this is like a halfway house. It is not wholly unknown, and I have a ready-made base of family and friends to welcome me in.

As I settle into the car, Stevie wedged into the back seat between me and Jude (although Gran had tried to insist she'd be fine in the back), I realise the tension I've been holding in my right shoulder for the last couple of weeks is no longer there. I look out of the window, seeing the sparkling sea, and happy holiday-makers, and the fishing boats and pleasure craft heading out now that the tide is in. When we park up and walk around towards Mum's apartment building, I go across to the railings and stop for a moment to watch and listen to the seawater sloshing against the harbour walls.

Stevie joins me. "Are you staying all summer?"

"I think so. Maybe even longer."

"Are you getting a job here?" she asks excitedly.

"I don't know!" I laugh. "I really have no idea what I'll be doing. But I will definitely be here for a while."

"That's sick," she says, which makes me smile.

"Are you going away this summer? On holiday?"

"I'm going with Granny up to see Julia and Paul and Angel."

"I can't believe they called their baby Angel!"

"I know. Mum thinks it's a bit out there and she says that Angel won't like it when she's growing up."

"She may have a point. But maybe it'll be cool."

"Yeah, I wouldn't mind having a name like that."

"Stevie's not too bad!"

"I guess."

"When you go to uni – if you want to go to uni – you can always reinvent yourself. You can become Stephanie. Or Steph?"

"I don't think so. I'm used to Stevie."

"Yeah, you're right. And it suits you."

"Come on, you two!" Mum is calling. "We've got a surprise for you, Ada."

"Really? What is it?"

"If I tell you it won't be a surprise, will it? Come and see for yourself!"

"Do you know what it is?" I turn to Stevie.

"Maybe." She is pressing her lips together in an attempt not to smile.

"Well, I can't wait any longer. Race you!" I say, and begin to run across the cobbled harbourside, careful not to trip up. Mum is holding the door open, and I walk into the open space of the ground floor of the building where she lives. Down here are commercial outlets and the community room. On the next floor up are offices. Mum's flat is right near the top, with beautiful views across the harbour and the estuary beyond.

"Ta-da!" Mum says, and steps aside to reveal a beautiful shining bike complete with basket and bell and adorned with a bright blue ribbon.

"Is that for me?" I ask, my eyes lighting up.

"Who else? Your own set of wheels!" Mum says, putting her arm round me. "Of course you can borrow my car when you need to as well, as long as I'm not using it. But I know you've missed cycling and I thought this might be a fun way for you to get about, or just do a bit of exploring."

"It's amazing! Thank you, Mum."

"It was Jude who got it actually," Mum says, and Jude smiles a little shyly.

"Somebody I knew was looking to get rid of it," she says, "so it's not brand new, sorry."

"As if that matters!" I say. "And it looks brand new anyway."

"Ah yes, one of the guys at the hub likes to do a bit of bike maintenance so he fixed it up. I think he's done a cracking job."

"He has! I love it. Thank you!"

"You can't keep it here of course," says Mum, "but there's a bike shed in the car park so we can put it in there and keep it locked safely away. Anyway, that's not all," she says excitedly.

"Really?"

"Really. Come on, let's go on up."

We all get in the lift, which is a bit of a squeeze, and I have a momentary fear of the lift breaking down and us all being stuck in it. Thankfully we reach Mum's floor unharmed and as the lift doors open I see there are balloons on her door.

"I did them!" Stevie says excitedly then remembers she is now a cool teenager and should play it down a bit. "Hope you like them."

"I do!" I say. "I really do."

Gran takes my arm as we go through Mum's front door and I see that the table is laid out with plates of sandwiches, cakes, crackers, cheese, grapes, and even some scones, cream and jam. A banner reading 'Welcome Home' is strung on the wall behind the table, as well as some more balloons.

"Oh this is so lovely. Thank you," I say, and I feel like crying.

"Well, we know it's not your home as such, or at least it might not feel like it. We wanted to make sure you know just how happy we are to have you here," says Mum.

I'm struck by how happy she looks, and how healthy. Her once pale skin is glowing and she's filled out a bit, but it suits her. And this open, expansive attitude she has these days is new, too. I put it down to a combination of Cornwall, and Jude, and no longer doing that all-consuming job that used to be her life.

"Come and see your room!" Stevie says, her eyes shining. She pulls at my arm.

"OK!" I laugh. "I'm coming!"

In the second of the two bedrooms, Mum has made the bed with some of my old covers, from when we lived in London. She's also hung up some of the pictures I had in my old room.

"Close the curtains," instructs Stevie.

I do as I'm told. On the ceiling, a hundred stars glow against the darkness.

"Just like your old room," Mum smiles. "And I know, I know, you're older now, and you might want to change things round. But I just wanted you to feel at home. I want this to feel like home."

"It does, Mum, thank you." I hug her. It will take a while longer for it really to feel anything like home but I'm so touched by the effort she's put in.

Stevie opens the curtains and I am struck by the view of the shimmering, dancing sea but I don't have long to admire it.

"Look up there on the wall!" Stevie says. I follow her gaze and see a wall-mounted TV. "And look! A drink machine!" She points to the recess of the built-in wardrobes and there, sure enough, is a coffee machine, stocked with pods for coffee and hot chocolate. "And a fridge!" She opens one side of the wardrobe.

"Bloody hell!" I laugh. "This is like some weird combination of my old bedroom and a hotel! Is there a safe tucked away somewhere?"

"Do you like it, though?" Mum asks anxiously.

"Mum, I love it. I am being well and truly spoiled and I don't think I deserve it!"

"Of course you do! And just the fact that you think otherwise is proof of that. I just… I know you're not going to be as independent as you were at university, and I know you're not even returning to the home you grew up in. I want you to feel as comfortable and at home here as you did there."

"Well, I think you've surpassed yourself. Thank you."

"I'm just so pleased to have you here, for as long as you want to stay. OK?"

"More than OK."

"Anyone for a cuppa?" Jude calls, and we trail out of my room and into the living area. Gran is taking layers of cling film from the plates of food and Jude is pouring tea from a pot.

"This is so, so nice," I say. I sink onto the settee and stare out of the floor-to-ceiling windows which open onto a tiny balcony. Mum's rearranged the furniture in here, so that the view is unobstructed.

"I'll get you a plate," Jude says, "if you don't mind."

"Mind?" I laugh. "Why would I mind being waited on hand and foot? And to think I expected Josh to be the one with servants!"

"Hey, less of the servant business!" Jude grins.

"So how is Josh?" Mum asks and I realise I didn't answer her earlier.

"He's alright," I say. "The same as me, really. I think we're all feeling it, the end of uni. It's weird, isn't it? The final year is so hard and all-consuming, and then all of a sudden, it drops away."

"I can't wait till I go," says Stevie.

"Yes, you're going to love it," I smile at her.

"Is he still coming to visit?" Mum asks, not wanting to drop the subject of Josh.

"Yes, I think so. And maybe... perhaps Archie might come too."

"Oh, really? I don't know if we'd be able to squeeze them both in."

"Not at the same time as Josh," I say. "And it's not definite. Just maybe."

"OK. Well of course, your friends are welcome here."

"We can always put people up at my house as well," Gran says.

"I don't like the idea of you having strangers staying with you, Mum," my mum says.

"He's not a stranger," I protest. "He's my friend. And he's lived with Josh all through uni."

"Yes, but we don't know him. Not really. We know Josh though."

I feel my hackles have risen a little, at this perceived slight on Archie. Plus, I want to know he can come and stay if he'd like to. I mean, Josh is one thing, and I can't wait for him to come to Cornwall, but the thought of having Archie here feels quite different and I can't help but think how romantic it could be. I want Mum to be as open to him coming to visit as she is to Josh.

I shake the idea from my head.

"We'll work it out," Jude says diplomatically, handing me a plate piled high with sandwiches, half a cheese-and-onion pasty, and some cherry tomatoes which are threatening to roll off onto the floor. "You must be tired," she says, smiling at me.

"I am," I say, and I realise it's true. I'm so tired. It's been non-stop work and then end-of-uni parties and then the weekend at Josh's.

"Now you can just relax for a bit," says Gran, putting her hand on my arm. "Just take some time to breathe and the plans will take care of themselves."

I smile at her and pop a cherry tomato into my mouth.

"From my garden," Gran says.

"It's lovely," I smile.

And we sit and chat and eat our lunch, finishing off with more tea and scones spread thickly with jam and clotted cream.

"I don't think I can eat another thing," I say, patting my full stomach contentedly.

"Maybe you want a lie down this afternoon?" Mum suggests.

"Do you know what? That sounds perfect," I say.

Stevie looks a bit disappointed but I realise that yes, a lie down, and a bit of time to myself to just let everything wash and settle over me, might be exactly what I need.

"Thank you, Mum," I say, kissing her before heading into my room. "For everything."

"It is my pleasure, believe me."

2016

Two years after their first visit to Cornwall together, Ada and Clara returned, this time with no Louisa.

"My goodness, girls," said Elise, "I can't get over how grown-up you are. Sorry, I know that's the kind of things adults always say! But it's true. My age must be catching up with me, though."

These days, Elise was spending a lot more time doing, well, very little, although she was not about to let on to anyone about that, least of all her granddaughter. But the thought of this visit had carried her through the last couple of months, following on from a lonely winter.

The girls both hugged Elise and then looked around them, delighted to be back. This time, they'd brought one giant rucksack each, which had made them feel like they were going inter-railing. They'd stood together on the platform at Paddington, having taken the tube to get there, and both were doing their best to appear more confident than they felt. Together, though, they felt they could do anything.

Now, they walked either side of Elise, and they seemed so tall to her. Had she shrunk? Maybe, but they'd definitely been doing some growing as well.

With a full face of makeup, Clara looked about eighteen and Ada not far behind.

"I can't wait to get in the sea!" Clara exclaimed.

"Well, it's ready and waiting for you," said Elise.

"Oh, I think we should spend some time with you first, Gran," said Ada.

"Don't you worry about me!" chuckled Elise. "I'm just glad to have you here. Let's get home and you can get changed into your swimming costumes and off you go."

'Swimming costumes' didn't quite cover it, she soon realised, when Clara swanned into the room in a white bikini and see-through kimono-style dress. Ada was wearing a pair of denim cut-offs and a t-shirt with a slashed neck which fell open over a shoulder, and it was clear her swimwear would not be much more modest than Clara's, although Elise was glad she had covered up a little more for the walk to the beach. Once she got there, Elise knew, there wouldn't be much covering up, but that was what they were all wearing these days, and it didn't mean anything. It just still took a bit of getting used to, having been brought up to keep covered up. She remembered her mortification at wearing one of her long-ago employer Lady Camelford-Bassett's costumes in front of his lordship; how she had been glad of Tabitha as a shield against the shape of her body. But it wasn't anything to be ashamed of, she thought; she just wasn't convinced it was anything to be showing off, either. But times had changed.

"Do you need towels?" she asked.

"No, we're all set," said Ada, patting the drawstring bag slung over her shoulder.

"Off you go then," Elise smiled. "I'll have some sandwiches ready for you if you let me know when you're coming back. No rush."

"Thanks Gran," Ada said, kissing her. The girl's eyes were alight and laughing, and Elise was touched when she doubled back to hug her again. "It's so good to be here."

"It is so good to have you here." Elise smiled to herself and crossed the room to her chair in the window. She'd left the paper open on the arm, the crossword half-completed. Now she could finish it; it paid to keep her mind sharp and not let herself get too old. She would not allow herself to drift off into old age without a bit of a fight.

The week flew by. The girls slept in late most mornings and Elise would have eggs for them, or veggie bacon, which she tried and thought was fairly palatable, and bread she had baked herself. Ada found herself a little bit torn between family loyalty, knowing that she should spend time with her gran, and the excitement of her first holiday without her mum. Just her and Clara – well, and the group of sixteen-year-old boys from Exeter, who had not long finished their GCSEs and were camping nearby.

Clara had hit it off with Tommy, the tallest one, and she talked about him incessantly. With his blue eyes, spiky blond hair and tanned skin, he was very good-looking, thought Ada, but he was so loud and seemed a bit too determined to have a good time. She preferred the quieter, darker Liam, who had a girlfriend back home but who seemed happy to spend time with Ada.

They didn't mention the boys to Elise of course, and Ada felt a bit uneasy about it. Her gran was so trusting but they were keeping a secret from her, and Clara had been drinking, too. Ada wasn't too fussed about drink; Louisa was far too reliant on her wine, in her opinion, and she was determined not to go the same way. Still, it was undeniably fun having a group of boys to swim with and play volleyball with, and to lie next to on the beach. Liam had helped with her suncream more than once, rubbing it smoothly into her back.

Ada had watched Clara push aside the straps of her bikini, encouraging Tommy to slide his hands under them, which he more than happily did, rubbing the cream over Clara's shoulders and onto her chest. Clara smiled. Ada felt uncomfortable and looked away.

In the evenings, the girls would cook for Elise and while Ada felt like they should stay in with her, maybe play some board games or cards, Elise insisted that if they wanted to go out they could, as long as they weren't back too late and as long as their parents didn't mind.

So the girls would wash up and clean the kitchen and then off they'd go to the campsite to find the boys, and on the last night Clara disappeared off inside a tent with Tommy. Ada was aware suddenly that she was essentially alone with five lads she didn't really know. It felt a little bit scary but also empowering. The only girl there, they wanted her attention and told her stories of bands they'd been to see, how they thought they'd done in their exams, and where and what they were hoping to study next. Their plans for the future and maybe next year going inter-railing.

"You should come with us!" Liam said.

"Oh yeah, Amy would love that," snorted Damian.

When Clara and Tommy emerged from the tent, both of them grinning a little sheepishly, Ada stood up. "Come on, we'd better get back to Gran."

Clara rolled her eyes, which annoyed Ada but she knew her friend was just showing off.

"It's our last night, and I want to make sure I spend some time with her."

"Alright," said Clara, and she gave Tommy a long, lingering kiss.

Liam stood up and awkwardly hugged Ada. "If I wasn't going out with Amy…" he whispered in her ear.

She just smiled. "Well, you are," she said. "But it's been lovely hanging out with you."

"Keep in touch?" he asked.

"I don't think Amy would be too pleased about that," she suggested.

"I can pass messages on!" Clara suggested, "Liam can tell Tommy and he can tell me."

"Sure," said Tommy, and he winked at Ada. She looked away.

As they left the campsite, Clara clasped Ada's hand. "You'll never guess what I've done!"

"I think I already have," said Ada.

"I'll tell you all about it later."

"You don't have to," said Ada but, seeing Clara's face, she relented. "You know you can tell me anything! Friends first, remember?"

"Of course."

Ada

The day after arriving in Cornwall, I sleep till lunchtime. I awake to the familiar sound of gulls and for a moment I think I am in my old student bedroom. I pull my senses and memory together and remember that all of that is behind me. I am now in Cornwall.

Voices from outside my door tell me that both Mum and Jude are out there. I am glad of the en suite bathroom so I can shower and freshen up a bit before going out there and having to be sociable. I suppose I haven't met Jude many times, despite her and Mum having been together a couple of years so, although I really do like her (I know it sounds like I'm trying to convince you or even convince myself), it still takes some energy. I am not yet one hundred per cent relaxed in her presence. Now that I am here, I have the perfect opportunity to rectify that, and I fully intend to. But just for now, I will take my time.

It's a new thing for me, seeing my mum with a partner. I do like it, but it's taking some getting used to. I know she has had a few relationships since I came along, though I am sure she thought I was unaware of them. One in particular I remember; I think he was somebody from work, and it wasn't all that long ago. I saw them kissing one night, at our gate, but when Mum came in I pretended I was asleep so she has no idea that I saw them. I remember she seemed really happy, perhaps more than I'd ever known her to be. But now, I think, she is even happier. As far as I know, Mum has not been with a woman before Jude but then again perhaps she was better at hiding things than I give her credit for.

What's odd about it is how I fit into things. Would it be better or worse if we were in our old house? Would I slot back into my own space and feel instantly at ease, or would I resent somebody else coming into our home – putting the TV on, or helping themselves to things in the kitchen? I'll never know now, and it feels like the onus is on me to fit into their lives rather than the other way round. No doubt I'm a little bit on edge and sensitive to this new situation, and mourning the life I've just left behind me. That was only ever meant to be temporary, transient, but I did love it.

Once I've showered and dressed, and wrapped a towel around my hair, I emerge into the flat to find Mum alone.

"Hi," I say, looking around for Jude.

"Hello my love, have a good sleep?" Mum has never called me 'my love'. She must be slipping back into her Cornish heritage.

"Yes thanks."

"Jude put some coffee on when she heard the shower going. She's gone back to her place now though."

"Oh that was nice of her. The coffee, I mean."

"She's worried it's strange for you, her being around right now. I think she's right. I want to spend the week with you, and Mum as well. Would you like that?"

"I would," I smile. "I really would." I'm immediately grateful to Jude for her thoughtfulness. I don't know whether Mum would have considered this if it wasn't for her. Love her as I do, she's not always the most emotionally intelligent about things.

I sip the coffee, which is strong and black, and Mum makes us some toasted pitta breads filled with avocado and egg, and slices of salted tomato with crunchy sea salt and freshly picked basil leaves.

"Mum, you're cooking!" I say teasingly.

"Well, sort of!" she smiles good-naturedly. "Working at the food bank's made me see things a bit differently. I mean, I still shop at M&S, but those ready-made things are so wasteful. I get some of the excess from the food bank too, when there is any. Honestly, some weeks it's amazing what we're given. Not all the fresh fruit and veg, and bread, can be given away, so we get what's left."

"I'm impressed," I say. "And this is delicious."

Mum smiles. I notice her freckles have come out. I don't think I ever noticed her freckles while we lived in London but since she's been here, they seem to appear at the lightest touch from the sun. It suits her. She has wrinkles too, but despite this her face looks smoother somehow. No doubt a product of the extra weight she is carrying, which has rounded off some of her sharper angles, but I also think it's this slower pace of life, and the relief of all those work hassles having been lifted from her shoulders.

"How is it, being here?" she asks.

"I don't even know yet!" I laugh.

"No, I suppose you don't. Just take your time to settle in. If you want to do something later, let me know. A

walk on the beach, a visit to Gran; trip to the shops –
whatever you fancy. Or we can do absolutely nothing.
Just see what you feel like."

I'm so glad, and so grateful, that the pressure has been
lifted from me too. It will take some adjusting to, this
new situation, and I'm very fortunate that the people
around me seem to understand that.

2019

The holidays in Cornwall became an annual event. Ada and Clara looked forward to them all year long, through the wet days tramping to school, dodging puddles and trying to avoid being splashed by cars.

The girls finished their GCSEs and decided to go on to the same college together, Ada to study art, sociology and English Literature; Clara took English Lit too, alongside history and politics. She also took up with a boy called James who was in her politics class and the two friends merged into a larger group, going out to bars and gigs on the weekends and working part-time jobs in cafes, shops and pubs to fund their social lives.

Louisa, keen to furnish Ada with more cultural experiences, took her on weekends away to Florence and Rome and Paris, where they'd spend their time in museums and art galleries, restaurants and shops. It was nice, having her mum to herself, Ada reflected; she knew that Clara was struggling with her relationship with her own mum, convinced that Lily was the favourite and Harry the golden boy, and that Mary had taken a dislike to James, all because she didn't want him staying over.

"I bet your mum would let you have boys stay over," Clara said to Ada.

"I don't know. I've never asked. I've never wanted to," Ada admitted.

It was true. She had not yet met a boy she liked enough. But she did have a secret crush, that she had not told even Clara about. And it was certainly not somebody Louisa would have allowed to stay over.

Mr Noble – "Call me Ben" – was twenty-seven and had been an art teacher for five years. He loved teaching A-Level students, and he loved his fiancée, who he was planning to marry in the summer.

Tall and well built, with messy dark hair and a smattering of stubble, nevertheless it wasn't so much his looks as his easy, encouraging manner which drew his pupils to him; his enthusiasm for creating, and self-expression, and following your own path in life. Not to mention those deep, dark, long-lashed eyes.

Given his tendency to cast himself as a free spirit, a more cynical person might have questioned his steady relationship with the same girl he'd been with since the age of sixteen, his millstone mortgage, and his weekend visits to a priest for 'marriage lessons'. But Ada was not that person, and she fell for him headfirst.

To be fair to Mr Noble – Ben – until Ada, he had never even considered acting on any desires. Yes, he'd enjoyed the attention he got but these were kids; sixteen, seventeen, eighteen. They were young, enthusiastic, sometimes pretentious, often loveable – but only ever in a fraternal kind of way. And then there was Ada Morgan.

She seemed older than her years, and she was thoughtful. She was also very pretty, but that was by the by. No, Ben felt, it was her spirit which drew him to her. She looked at the world in a certain way and she expressed it all so well. He had never taught any other student who could capture a person's essence in their work the way she could, in their eyes or the slightest lift at the corner of a mouth.

While the others were experimenting with abstracts and still-lifes and shapes and landscapes, Ada was set on creating characters; real people and imagined. And then one day she drew him.

She was alone in the classroom one lunchtime and she was so intent on her work that she hadn't heard him come in.

"Is that...?" he asked, seeing immediately what she was doing.

She blushed, very fetchingly, and stuttered, "I was just... I..."

"It's very good," he said, trying his best to be objective, and not acknowledge the compliment.

"I just wanted to try drawing somebody from memory." Her face was a dark red now, her embarrassment almost tangible.

"Well, I... it's great, Ada. Really great." He put his hand on her arm. Had she flinched then? He withdrew it quickly. "I don't mean me. I don't mean I'm great!" He laughed, and felt nervous suddenly, seeing her eyes on him; even now she seemed to be taking in details. "If it wasn't... well, me... I'd suggest submitting it as one of your pieces."

"I think that might look inappropriate," she had smiled, suddenly, and it was like the sun breaking out from behind a cloud.

"I can always sit for you if you like," he said. "One weekend."

"You mean, like, a life drawing?" her face was very serious.

"God, no!" he started, then he looked at her, saw her smiling. "You're joking."

"Yes. I'm joking. That really would be inappropriate."

"I should say so."

There was a knock at the door and there stood Amber Jones, Ben's teenage sweetheart and present-day fiancée, who worked at the doctors' surgery nearby. The two of them would often meet to eat their lunch together, either outside on the grass or sitting in their car if it was raining.

"I thought you were on your way," Amber said. "Sheila let me come in to find you."

"Amber!" Ben said; almost too quickly, Ada thought, and she casually placed one of her other pieces of work over the picture of Ben. He glanced back towards her and saw what she was doing. He smiled gratefully, she thought. "Sorry. Let me just grab it. I'll be right out."

"Honestly, you said you'd be straight out!" Amber smiled at Ada and rolled her eyes. "Men!"

Ada just smiled back. Ada watched Amber put her arm through Ben's and she was sure he chanced a very quick glance back across his shoulder, then they were out of sight and she was alone once more. She pulled her picture out again and ran a critical eye over it. She hadn't quite got his mouth right, she saw, but her concentration had been broken now and she decided to head outside to find Clara and the others.

Ada

By mid-week, all best intentions have started to go awry. It is so obvious that Mum and Jude are missing each other and Mum talks about Jude so much that I end up saying exasperatedly to just call her and get her to come over. I'm fighting my urge to cringe at how much in love she seems to be. I am happy for her, I really am, but it's kind of weird, seeing her behave around Jude like Charlotte does around Will. It makes me wonder how Sasha is getting on with Andrew too. I wonder if she's still at Josh's. I'm secretly hoping that Mum will decide to go to Jude's house but, ever the control freak, I think she is more comfortable in her own space. "Jude's is a bit like a student hovel!" she laughs when I ask her about it. "Books and dust everywhere."

I think of my own shared house, which I still can't believe is empty and waiting patiently for the next crop of students. It wasn't like the kind of place you'd see on *The Young Ones*, or even on *Fresh Meat*. There were no dusty, crumbling walls, no dodgy landlords, not even a weird housemate (unless that was me and I was oblivious to the fact). I have to fight the yearning to be back there.

So after just three days Jude is back, and it's not her I have a problem with. It's Mum who begins to annoy me. She is always checking that Jude's alright, and she is almost apologetic on my behalf if I've left any of my things lying around or a teabag sitting in its own mess in the sink.

"It's fine!" Jude reassures her. "This is Ada's home."

But it doesn't feel like it to me.

And now that Mum's got over her relief and delight at having me back she's started to bring in her 'ground rules', about living here. I understand that we need to have some understanding between ourselves. I'm much more used to living in shared accommodation than she is, in fact. But as soon as she starts to mention me needing to get some work, and the fact that I will be living here rent-free but I will need to contribute, and maybe we'll have a cleaning rota, and cooking rota, and… I can feel my teenage self begin to wake from its not-so-long slumber.

"Alright, alright," I want to say. "I get it. Just stop going on about it." Instead, I retreat in what I hope is a dignified manner to my bedroom and pull out my sketch book. I'm trying to hold on to the ideas which came to me at Josh's house, and to build on them. Something good is brewing, I'm sure of it, but I don't yet know what direction it is going to take.

Mum sees my withdrawal as my going off and sulking but I really am trying to be diplomatic, to give her and Jude some space, and to avoid arguments at all cost.

If I am being reasonable, I imagine it must be taking Mum some adjusting as well. She has been through a lot of change these last few years, from me effectively leaving home, her losing her job and moving here, to her relationship with Jude, and my returning again. I try to remember all this but it's not always easy. Luckily I also have Gran's house to go to, and I do most days.

"Just come and go as you please," Gran has said. "And if you need some work space, you've got my attic. It's not like I can get up there these days myself so it's all yours. I won't be able to see what you're getting up to!" She has a twinkle in her eye when she says this.

"Do you miss it?" I ask.

"What, getting up to mischief?"

"No!" I laugh. "The painting. Creating. The... being able to get up into the attic."

"I suppose I do," she muses, "but it's best not to dwell on it. I've been very fortunate, much luckier than many, to have been so mobile for so long. But it's catching up with me. It had to sometime, you know."

I look at her hands, which are swollen and stiff. I consider everything those hands have done in their time. The hard manual labour of raising a family not long after the war, and the endless hours of typing she told me she had to do at the law firm where she worked with her friend Maudie. The painting, too – she's done some lovely work, has Gran, but only for her own benefit, she says. I've told her she should show it to some of the local galleries, but she won't hear of it.

"Anyway, what are your plans, Ada? Now you've finished your degree and you're stuck here with us oldies?"

"I really don't know, long-term. But I do need to earn some money. I think I'll see if they need any more lifeguards over the summer."

"Well, a summer on the beach doesn't sound too bad. And it'll do you good to get to know some young folk round here. I bet you're missing your friends."

"I really am," I say.

"And is your friend still coming to visit?"

"Josh?"

"Not Josh, the other one."

"Archie?" I ask, blushing and knowing that sharp-eyed Gran won't have missed it.

"That's the one. Archie."

"I…" The truth is, I'm not sure. We've been messaging on and off, and I am building up to asking him if he still wants to come over to Cornwall. He's back at his parents' now, catching up with his old school friends and 'generally dossing about' as he put it. I've seen him tagged in a lot of Instagram posts at a bar that his friend runs, and he looks like he's having a ball.

"You like him?" Gran asks now.

"Erm. Yes, I do. I think."

"Is he as nice as Josh?"

"He's different. I don't know if nice is the right word."

"Ah," she says, knowingly.

"What?" I can't help laughing.

"It's never the nice ones, is it? Nice isn't enough for us!"

"But Josh isn't… it's not like that with me and him."

"But it is with you and Archie?" she says, triumphantly, like she's caught me out.

"I don't know. I do like him, I guess. Josh and me, we're like best friends. Archie is…"

"A dish?"

Now I really am laughing, and so is she. "That's it, Gran. He's a dish. A dreamboat."

110

"Look, my love. You're young. Things are different to how they were in my day. If you like this Archie and he likes you, then I don't see that there's any harm in asking."

"I suppose so," I say, and I know she's right. I mean, for god's sake, it's the 21st century. I can ask Archie out, or at the very least see if he still wants to come and visit, and we can take it from there. What have I got to lose?

"I know so," she says firmly.

I wait until later, when I'm on my way job-hunting, to message Archie. I pluck my phone from my pocket, quickly tap out: **Still want to come and visit?** I add **X** for good measure, then I switch my phone to silent and head to the RNLI HQ, which is a little further along the harbourside from Mum's place. I know they're looking for Grade 1 beach lifeguards, which is the same level I worked at last summer, staying on in my uni flat with Sasha, Pippa and Rachael at various different times, according to when they were on their trips round Europe, and family holiday to the Maldives in Pippa's case.

I'm so grateful to Gran for keeping me interested in swimming when I was younger. It was something she had been pushed to do when she was at school, and she says she never regretted it.

"I remember going to the Whiteleys interview with my mum," Gran has told me, Whiteleys being the all-girls' school she went to; the one that was evacuated here, to Tregynon Manor. "They asked then if I could swim and I hadn't the first clue how to. At the original school, we had use of a pool, and then when we came here we were able to carry on with swimming lessons. The beaches were out of bounds, except for supervised weekend walks, and it wasn't until I was a bit older that I could swim in the sea but I'll never forget my first time, and how glad I was that I was a strong swimmer."

While Gran didn't interfere at all with my childhood, or with Mum's choices – or at least not as far as I'm aware – this was the one area where she spoke up, and she paid for my lessons even though Mum was quite adamant she didn't have to, but Gran said she wanted to. I took my pool lifeguard course as soon as I could and then my beach one, during my first year at uni. Now Gran has put me onto this opening at the local RNLI, as she knows someone who knows someone... that's very often how it works round here.

I knock on the door and hear a voice tell me to push it open so I do as I'm told. "Give it a good shove!" I hear, and I do, and the door flies open. I have to stop myself falling into the room. A tanned man in a RNLI jacket is looking through some files on a shelf. "Hello?" he turns and smiles.

"Hi. Are you Wes?"

"That's me. You must be Ava?" I am reminded instantly of Antonia.

"Ada," I correct him.

"Ada. Sorry. I should have remembered that, as in Ada Lovelace."

"Yes! That's who I was named after."

"Are you a computer wizard as well?"

"I definitely wouldn't say that."

"All you kids are, compared to my generation! Sorry," he says again, "I shouldn't be calling you kids. Now, have you got your form with you? And your certificates?"

"Yes," I wave a folder at him.

"Excellent, excellent. We could do with somebody starting sooner than later, you know. Been a bit let down by one of our crew and everyone's having to do extra shifts to fill in at the moment."

"Sorry to hear that."

"Yeah, well, he's following his dreams, in Hawaii of all places. Some surf competition or other. I'm a bit jealous, truth be told, though my knees can't take the surfing these days."

He's talking like he's Gran's age, or Mum's at the very least, but I reckon Wes can only be in his thirties.

"I'm happy to start as soon as you need me," I tell him. "I'm back for the summer, maybe longer."

"Smashing. Well, we're definitely in need of somebody till the end of September. Possibly longer. Will that suit you, Ada?"

"That will suit me just fine."

"Great, well let me take those—" I hand him my certificates – "and I can take some copies. Then if you could drop in for an interview tomorrow morning – meet our senior, Charlie, and maybe another one of the team – hopefully we can offer you some work. About eleven?"

"That's brilliant! Thank you."

"No worries. But I shouldn't have said that, really, not till you've had your interview. I'm not the best at this official stuff, I'll be honest, so don't take it as read until we've offered you a position, OK?"

"OK!" I grin.

I wait until I'm out of the door before taking my phone from my pocket to see if Archie has responded. My heart skips to see that he has, and that he has responded

113

positively – **Love to** – and not only that but he's reciprocated with not one but three kisses. **XXX**. Pathetic it may be, but it puts a spring in my step. I bound up the stairs to Mum's flat and find her alone in the kitchen.

"I've got a job!" I say excitedly. "Well as good as. I just have to meet a couple of the other lifeguards tomorrow."

"That's wonderful, Ada! Well done. It will buy you some time while you decide what you want to do next."

"And I'll contribute to the household expenses. I really don't mind paying rent you know," I say earnestly.

She smiles. "We can discuss that side of things."

"Oh, and you know I mentioned about Archie coming to stay? Well he'd like to so I'm just going to give him a call to sort it out." I move to head into my room. I am so excited things are starting to come together.

"Hang on," she says. "I don't really know this Archie, do I? Where's he going to stay?"

"Erm… on the sofa?"

"I don't think that will work, really, do you?"

"Or he can have my room and I can sleep on the sofa. Or he and I can stay at Gran's."

"No. That won't work either. I don't want Mum having to put up somebody she doesn't know."

"It's just the same as what we're doing when Josh comes, though."

"Yes, but we know Josh, don't we?"

"And you'll know Archie when he comes."

There is a rumble of imminent disappointment within me.

"I don't know, Ada. Is this a romantic thing?"

"No!" I say, flushing. "Well, I don't know. It could be."

"Isn't Archie the boy that your friend Sasha was talking about when we went out for dinner?"

I think back to a time when Mum and Jude came to visit. They'd been in London to see a show, and to visit Bocca Felice, this Italian restaurant that Mum has been going to forever, before coming down to stay on the South Coast for a few days. When we were going out to eat one night, Mum invited Josh and Sasha along and yes, I remember Sasha was shooting her mouth off about Archie as well as a lot of other people. She does enjoy a good gossip, that girl. I can't believe Mum remembers that, though.

"I could tell you liked him then," Mum says. "The way you were defending him."

"Was I?" I don't really remember that.

"Yes. You're quite transparent sometimes, Ada!" Mum laughs, and I feel an immediate bubbling of rage.

"I'm twenty-two, Mum."

"Yes, twenty-two. A baby."

"Oh my god, I can't believe you've just said that."

"No, neither can I. I'm sorry." She does actually have the grace to look contrite. "I don't mean it like that. But I have been round the block a few times Ada, and I know what men are like. You don't agree with me about this, but there are certain types, you know."

"That's ridiculous!"

"Is it, though? Honestly, this Archie sounds like trouble."

"You've never even met him."

"No, but everything Sasha said about him…"

"You don't have to take everything Sasha says as gospel."

115

"And Josh…"

"What did Josh say?"

"Oh, I don't remember exactly." She is suddenly cagey.

"When did he say it? Go on, you must remember what he said, if you're so concerned."

"Oh, I don't know."

I am sure that Mum thinks I should get together with Josh. She absolutely loves him, as do I. But she's quite mistaken if she thinks there is something romantic going on there.

"Mum," I say, "Archie is my friend. Yes, I do like him, but we are not together. I would like to be able to invite him to stay because, well because I'm an adult and I should be able to do that. It was actually Gran who said I should ask him, anyway. So I'll see if we can stay at her house. If she says no, we can look for a B&B. Or go camping. It's not like there's a shortage of places to stay around here."

"Oh no, don't do that. I'm sorry, Ada. Of course you should ask him here."

"No. It's fine. Honestly, I don't want to do that when I know he won't be welcome. I'll sort something out, don't worry. I'm quite capable of looking after myself you know, Mum. I've been doing it all my life."

Now where did that come from? I regret it immediately, seeing the look on Mum's face. I know she feels like she was absent far too much while I was growing up – and when I was little I had a nanny, and childminder, so that Mum could work all the hours her job demanded of her – but I didn't really feel neglected. I could kick myself for such a low blow but it's out there now. "Sorry," I say. "I didn't mean that."

"It's fine," she says stiffly. "I suppose we're both finding it difficult to adjust to living together again. And I know, I do know, I need to give you your space, and respect your autonomy. Honestly, if you want Archie to come here, then ask him. We can sort something out. I can go and stay at Jude's."

I imagine Archie and me living in Mum's flat for a few days, like we're a grown-up, high-flying couple. The thought is appealing. He'd love this place, I know it. "No, thank you Mum, it's alright. I'll ask Gran. She's got two spare rooms, it'll be fine. And I'll make sure we don't put on her. Archie's a good person, you'll see."

She frowns but just shrugs her shoulders then pulls me to her for a hug. "Sorry for calling you a baby."

"Sorry for saying what I said," I mutter awkwardly, not wanting to repeat the words. "I really didn't mean it."

"I know. You were just kicking out, and for good reason. You're a great kid… young woman. I'm proud of you."

"And I'm proud of you," I say and I hug her tightly, feeling this strange mixture of being her child but of wanting to look after her too. I suppose it's what happens as you reach adulthood and begin to see your parents' vulnerabilities. Just as she wants to protect Gran, I want to protect her. If we can all look after each other then I think we will be alright.

2020

It was Ada's eighteenth birthday and the world was just coming to life again, tentatively, following endless weeks of total lockdown. In Ada's house it had been fairly peaceful but at times incredibly boring. Louisa was working on a project based coincidentally in the Cornish town she'd been brought up in and where her mum still lived; it was a huge concern, renovating existing warehouses, creating residential and commercial spaces.

For Ada, this space of time was all about her A-Levels. Online lessons did not go anywhere near replacing actual face-to-face learning, but she and Louisa ordered as many books as they could from Amazon, delighting in the doorbell ringing to break the monotony of the day. Ada read as much as she could, and looked for YouTube tutorials. She was damned if she was going to let a pandemic ruin her academic achievements. And she and Clara would be on video call to each other every day, sometimes studying English together and sometimes sunning themselves in their respective gardens, barely talking but still connected, so grateful that the weather was ridiculously good. And sometimes Ada would be listening to Clara wailing about how much she missed seeing James. How her parents wouldn't let him sneak across to their place, even on a dog walk, just to meet in their garden...

"But that's the way it is for everyone," Ada would say.

"But I love him!" Clara would say and Ada would shrug, pleased she didn't have a relationship to worry about.

Only at night did she let her mind drift towards Ben, and she'd check the messages he'd sent to her on Teams.

"Could I WhatsApp you?" he had asked. "So we can chat about your work more easily? No pressure."

"Of course," she'd replied, sending him her number, and now they were messaging each other multiple times a day, and his name would provoke a frisson of excitement within her.

Unbeknown to her, he felt the same. He was finding life at home a little bit stifling. Amber was obsessing about the wedding and what they were going to do, when nobody would be able to come, and he was finding he cared less and less. The messages from Ada were a high point in his day.

At least Amber, being frontline staff, was still required to go out to work, he thought a little guiltily. It provided them with respite from each other during the day. Even so, he felt bad when she came home with tales of distressed, disappointed, sometimes abusive, patients, stressed doctors, and overstretched hospitals. To make it up for her, he made sure he had tea ready and waiting, alongside a G&T, when she got home each night.

"I don't know what I'd do without you," she'd smile and kiss him, and he'd grin and shift a little uncomfortably.

It wasn't that he didn't love her, but all of this was getting a bit much. He didn't share her concerns about the wedding; in fact, he was beginning to think they were maybe a bit young for all this. Now life had been curtailed by necessity; now his freedoms had been removed, he was dreaming of alternative realities and some of these, he couldn't help noticing, involved Ada Morgan.

By the time her birthday came around, schools were back in, for a limited number of pupils. A-Level and

GCSE exams had been cancelled. Grades were to be decided by a 'moderated algorithm'. It was all very disappointing from an academic perspective but, Ada supposed, better than the alternative.

And her mum seemed happy; happier than she had in a long time. Ada heard Louisa laughing away on video calls with her colleagues, and it hadn't escaped her attention that 'AJ' was regularly dropped into conversation. She had never spent this much time with Louisa and it was turning out to be a lovely experience. It would have been a different story, she supposed, if they lived in a small flat, and didn't have an outside space; even if their family was larger. In addition to Clara missing James 'soooooo much', Ada's friend also had plenty of gripes about being stuck with all her family, all the time. Ada could imagine that might make the experience a little bit more trying, especially as Clara shared a room with Lily. Not having some personal space would be tricky.

During the most stringent lockdowns, Louisa and Ada had got into the habit of rising early and doing some yoga or trying to follow a Joe Wicks workout. Then they'd have breakfast and go their separate ways until lunchtime. Usually it would be a salad which they would eat sitting in the sunshine, then they'd brew up some coffee to keep them going through the afternoon and it would be back to work for them both.

Later, they might take the opportunity for their permitted limited daily exercise, strolling around the block, and the day would be rounded off with a film and a ready meal (not just any ready meal, this was an M&S ready meal, delivered by Ocado), and a glass of wine (or two) for Louisa. Really, Ada thought, life could be a lot worse.

She knew that Ben was struggling in the flat with Amber; he'd told her he was finding it difficult; missing college; missing teaching. Missing her. Ben had hesitated before sending that message, and he had deleted it from his end of the conversation immediately. In fact he deleted most of their messages between each other, just being careful to save ones relevant to Ada's education. Just in case.

But Amber, who had previously tended towards being a little bit nervous – a little bit jealous – really had settled since the lockdowns began. He had, she supposed, no possible way of cheating on her. In fact, he never had been unfaithful and her insecurities to this point had been unfounded. At first he'd gone out of his way to appease and reassure her but over the years her questioning of him had begun to grate.

"Why are you marrying me, if you don't trust me?" he had wanted to ask her, but never dared. He had begun to suspect that she would be happy if he was always kept at home, like this. Away from temptation. Little did she know.

Want to meet for a walk? he asked Ada one day, when limited mixing of households was allowed. He held his breath as he awaited her reply.

I don't know.

He exhaled. That was probably for the best. Then...

Actually, yes. That would be nice.

Shit. What was he getting himself into?

***

They decided to make it look like they'd just bumped into each other, walking around the park that was about halfway between their respective homes.

He sat on a bench and waited nervously and when he saw her he felt something he hadn't for years. Excited.

For her part, Ada was nervous and full of doubt. As she approached him, he made a big deal of being surprised to see her, which made both of them laugh.

"Mind if I walk with you?" he asked.

"Sure."

And so they walked, side by side, around the park, not once but three times. The grass in the centre had grown dry during the extended spell of warm weather, but the well-tended flower beds were full of colour, and the playground was moderately busy, though families and children were keeping their distance from each other.

"That's kind of sad," observed Ben. "Having to tell kids to stay away from each other."

"I know. It must be a weird experience when you're tiny."

"It's weird for us all," said Ben. "It's bloody wearing."

Ada risked a side-on look at him. His fine, straight nose, and his broad shoulders. The boys in her year paled in comparison to this man, and she looked at his

122

lips, wondering what it would be like to kiss him. Very different to the few kisses she'd shared with boys her own age, she thought. They were young and nervous but Ben... well, he was a man. He had experience. She shook the thought from her head.

"Are you alright?" he asked, smiling at her.

"Oh, yes, erm, fine," she said, cursing her blush for giving her away.

The back of his hand brushed hers; or had she imagined it? Maybe so, because his talk turned to her A-Level work and very soon he said he had to go. He had begun to look around furtively. She knew that he could be in trouble, not just from Amber but from the college, if they were seen together.

"Do this again?" he asked.

"Sure." She tried to sound nonchalant but there was nothing she would like more.

And so the walks became a regular thing, though never in the same place twice. And over time they found more secluded places that they could go, where they were unlikely to be recognised, although once, on a shady path between some trees on the heath, he pulled her down to the ground, behind some bushes.

"I'm so sorry," he whispered, his eyes on hers. "It's the head."

"What?"

"Mick... The head of the college, and his family."

"Oh my god," she mouthed, her heart beating fast and an almost uncontrollable urge to giggle bubbling up within her.

"No," Ben mouthed back, wide-eyed, but his mouth was stretching into a smile too.

They held their breath, listening to Ben's boss as he talked to his wife about a weird dream he'd had the night before. "I was performing on stage at Wembley," he was saying, and that had Ada and Ben in silent stitches. Once the danger had passed, they let their laughter go free, erupting in giggles, and then somehow they were hugging, and then their eyes met, and then their lips, and Ada thought she was in heaven.

It was a guilty Ben who stayed behind in the bushes, watching Ada to make sure she was safe as she wandered along the isolated path. Then he followed at a distance, feeling like a creep; what if somebody saw him emerging from the bushes and following this young girl? He saw her turn off through the gateway back onto the leafy road that led towards the high street, and then he was safe to think about what had just happened.

He sat on a bench and reflected on the situation he had got himself into. He must be mad. Cheating on Amber, with a student. But she wasn't just any student. She was Ada Morgan, and he thought that he might be really falling for her.

***

Throughout the summer, they met when they could, and once when Amber was at work Ben invited Ada to his flat but she said no, and he knew she was right. Their relationship consisted of covert walks and furtive, fervent kisses behind trees, beneath bridges, and at the top of railway embankments. There was a disused railway along which people would walk and cycle and this offered a multitude of private spots for anyone willing to find them. Ben and Ada were more than willing.

The wedding plans had been postponed to the following year, which had Amber in tears and Ben consoling her, although secretly he was glad. He was fooling himself that it was buying him time but the reality was he already shared a home with Amber, they had already committed to each other, and deep down he knew that he couldn't really convince himself that things were alright; the only person being fooled was Amber. And it felt very bad.

Ada

"Hello gorgeous!" Archie sweeps his left arm around my waist, drawing me in for a hug, and a kiss just above my ear. In his right arm is a bunch of flowers. I look at them, and he laughs. "They're not for you!"

I feel chastened.

He grins at me. "They're for your gran!"

"I should hope so too!" I say, keen to appear as though I had never even considered he'd have brought me flowers. "She'll love them."

"Are you sure she doesn't mind me staying there? I don't think I've ever stayed with anyone's grandmother before."

"She's not really like anyone else's grandmother," I say. "And she doesn't mind at all. I'm staying there too," I remind him.

"Of course. That's good. I've missed you."

"Have you?"

"Of course! I've missed everyone."

Again, I feel stupid, hoping that he'd missed me in particular. But I am quick to save face. I begin walking to the car park and he moves along beside me.

I turn to him as we walk. "I miss everyone too. It's weird, isn't it? The whole thing being over? In a couple of months there'll be a whole new bunch of students starting out. Living in our places."

"Yeah there will, but we've got to keep moving forward, haven't we?"

"I guess."

"I've been in and out of a few agencies in London, and closer to home. It's not a bad place to be."

"No, I suppose the south-east is where it's all going on."

"And yet here you are!"

"Here I am. The mild, mild west."

"Did you say you're working as a lifeguard?"

"Yep."

"Well don't get too comfortable with it, you know? You should think about coming to London in the autumn. That's where I'm going."

"Are you?" I think of the house where I grew up, with a slight ache of longing. I do miss London and I suppose I could go back but it won't be the same. I do believe it's time for something new. I just don't know what.

"Yeah, I've got a mate who works in set design and I should be able to get some work with him while I get myself set up."

"Doing...?"

"Freelance stuff, for the agencies I mentioned. Keep up!" He grins and nudges me.

"You're the one who needs to keep up," I say and sprint down the path towards the car.

"Unfair!" he pants when he reaches me where I'm waiting at the gate to the car park. "You had a head start. And you're not carrying anything."

"Well, if you'd brought those flowers for me, I'd be carrying them..."

127

"I'll get you your own flowers. I've got to charm your gran though, haven't I? Otherwise she might not let me stay."

"You've got a lot of charming to do," I say. "Don't forget we're eating out with my mum and her partner tonight as well."

"Water off a duck's back," Archie says. "Mums love me. Now which one of these is yours?"

I walk to Mum's car.

"You're joking!" he says.

"No, this is it. Mum's quite keen on her cars."

"I can tell."

"Hop in then!"

He does as he's told, slinging his bag onto the back seat. I'm keen to be in control and I enjoy watching his face as I make the roof open. It's really not a long drive to town but I want to make the most of it. I take the slightly longer route around the back roads, bringing us in towards the harbour.

"It's really nice here," Archie says.

"Yes," I agree. "It is."

"I can see why you like it."

"Good."

"But what about the art scene? I know people used to flock down this way but there can't be much going on these days."

"You'd be surprised." Actually, he probably wouldn't be. There is certainly a prospering local art scene but it's not exactly cutting edge, for the most part at least. Often it's people who are just making a gentle living, or who have already made their living and are now focusing on art as something to tide them over.

There are absolutely loads of galleries all over Cornwall, and in this part particularly in St Ives, which has been long renowned and celebrated for its thriving arts and culture, but I'm not convinced I could really get anywhere if I stay here. And to be honest I'm not quite sure exactly where I want to get anyway. A familiar feeling of unease dredges the bottom of my stomach as I contemplate what the future might bring for me, particularly in comparison to somebody like Archie, who already seems to have a plan.

Working for advertising agencies, though? Is that really his dream? Who knows? I suppose it would beat many of the alternatives.

We leave the car in its allotted space and walk round to the front of the building. I point up to Mum's balcony.

"That's where I live," I say. "When you're not here."

"Are we slumming it, then? Or is that your Gran's?" He points up to where Tregynon Manor sits sunning itself on the cliffs.

"Ha! Not quite. Although, actually, that is exactly where she lived when she first came to Cornwall. And she worked there, too." We walk companionably along the harbourside and I find myself telling Archie about Gran's past, and how she came to end up here.

"It's amazing, isn't it? How all that was happening not all that long ago." Archie stops and looks towards Tregynon again. "And now it's a hotel. I guess that's what's happened round here to so many places. Tourism is god."

"It kind of is. It kind of has to be. The fishing industry's not anywhere near what it used to be, though we do still have a fishing fleet here," I say proudly, and find myself feeling just a little bit like I belong here.

Now that I can introduce a newcomer to the town, I realise how much I know about it. "And the opportunities for young people are few and far between. The place where Mum lives is pretty new and it's generated a few jobs, in the offices and restaurants, but not nearly as many as they said it would. And Mum and Jude, well I'm sure they'll be glad to tell you all about it tonight, but Jude runs the foodbank and Mum's been working as a volunteer there. It's never been as necessary as it is now."

"Shit."

"I know."

"To think a few weeks ago we were living it up at Josh's country estate. It's a world away."

"A hundred worlds away," I say but I feel the need to stand up for Josh. "But Josh knows that."

"Yeah, he's just powerless to do anything about it. Oh," he says, his attention moving quickly to something else, "that ice cream place looks amazing. Can we get one?"

"I don't see why not."

So we stop and I look after his bag, and Gran's flowers, and Archie returns with two three-scoop ice creams and a huge grin on his face.

"That must have set you back about twenty quid!" I say.

"Not quite, but near enough. She was pretty fit though."

"Oh yeah?" My dreams of this being a romantic visit are fast fading.

"Well, yeah. A bit young for me, though. What about you, anyway? Any nice lifeguards you've got your eye on?"

The dreams all but disappear.

"No, not really. Rob's pretty fit but I'm fairly sure he's gay."

"Another reason to come to London," he says. "You'll be living like a nun round here."

"I don't know about that! Or that it'd be any different in London." My mind flickers briefly to Ben Noble. I push those memories aside.

"We'll see."

I barely make a dent in my ice cream and in the end Archie 'has to' finish it for me.

"Why are you not the size of a house?" I laugh.

"Just got a super-fast metabolism," he says. "I've started running, too."

"You? Running?"

"Yeah, some of my mates back home are proper gym freaks and they've got me into it."

"Bloody hell. I don't think I saw you break into a sweat at uni."

"It did happen occasionally. But from a different kind of exercise." He smiles at me and annoyingly I feel my cheeks redden. "Got you! I knew I could make you blush."

"It's just the sun on my skin." I can't help smiling back.

"Sure."

"Come on," I stand up. "Gran's going to be waiting for us."

As we approach Godolphin Terrace I start to worry. What if Gran doesn't like Archie? It is a bit of an imposition, asking her to have us both to stay, and I wonder if Mum was right, that I shouldn't be putting on her in this way.

But she's always loved it when Clara's been with me. Is it so different that this time it's a boy I'm bringing back?

"Hello!" she says, as she answers the door, opening it wide and matching the gesture with her smile. "You must be Alfie."

He looks a little awkward.

"You know it's Archie!" I laugh. "Don't wind him up!" I relax a little. Maybe he'll have met his match with her.

"Sorry, Archie," she says, "I thought I'd play the confused-old-lady card. You are very welcome. Come on in."

She stands back, graciously accepting the flowers he hands to her. "These are lovely, thank you. Ada, can you get a vase for them, please?"

I can't help noticing how slow she is on her feet and as she walks behind us back into the lounge she sinks gratefully into her chair by the window.

"Are you alright, Gran?" I ask her. "You sound like you're breathing a bit heavily."

"Oh, I'm fine. Just my flower allergy, you know…" She looks at Archie with a wicked grin on her face. "Just kidding, Alfie! No, I just get a bit like this sometimes, I'm getting on, you know. It happens to us all, or those of us who are lucky enough to get to my age."

"How old are you?" Archie asks, and I remember this is one of the reasons I like him. He's unapologetically open and doesn't try to tread on eggshells around people.

"Well, you know they say you should never ask a lady her age. But I say that's a load of bobbins. I'm ninety-four, thank you for asking."

"That's awesome!" Archie says.

"I suppose it is. I've seen lots of people fall by the wayside, some far younger than me. So I know I'm lucky."

"And you've looked after yourself as well," I call through from the little kitchen as I cut the flower stems at angles before filling the vase with water and trying to arrange the flowers artistically. "How are these?" I ask, carrying them through and setting them on the windowsill.

Archie, a very well-brought-up boy as it turns out, insists on making us cups of tea, so I show him where everything is. In the tight space of the kitchen I am aware of the proximity of our bodies and at one point, as he reaches across for the milk, he puts his hand gently on the small of my back. I try not to react in any way. He smells of something like sandalwood, and I remember the array of his aftershaves in the bathroom he shared with Josh and Jack.

"Alright?" he asks me.

"Yes, yes. It's nice to have you here."

"It's nice to be here." He is just inches away, smiling right at me, and I recall that moment in the lake at Josh's. He was going to kiss me then, wasn't he? Or did I imagine it?

"Let's take this through," I say awkwardly, grabbing a tray and a packet of biscuits from the counter.

We sit side by side, me sipping my tea and watching Archie munch his way through three biscuits while he makes pleasant conversation with Gran. It seems I need not have worried about him making a good impression and I can tell that she likes him.

When he excuses himself to go to the bathroom she says, "He's very nice, and he's very good looking."

"I can't say I'd noticed."

She laughs loudly. "I'm sure. Just enjoy yourself, my love. You're young. He's a nice boy, I can see that. Just have some fun."

I smile at her but then we hear the toilet flush so we quickly change the subject to our plans for the evening.

2020

When A-Level results day came around, Louisa had decided to take the day off work. Although by this point people were being allowed, even encouraged, to go on holiday (although not abroad), both Ada and Louisa had agreed that it was better to stay put. They'd heard from Elise that Cornwall was full to bursting and that some of the locals were up in arms, terrified that their public services were about to be brought to the knees by Covid; others, Elise said, were just glad that there was going to be some trade this year.

"But if I were you, I'd stay put. Don't come here, Ada. Not yet. Maybe in the autumn."

"Maybe. But I'll be working by then, all being well."

"Of course you will! Well, we'll work something out."

Clara had been very disappointed; she'd been counting on getting away for a bit.

"I'm really sorry," said Ada. "But I don't think it would be fair on Gran."

"I guess," Clara said. "I mean, I know it's right but I really could do with a break."

"I know you could. At least you can see James a bit more now."

"Yeah, but I think maybe that's run its course."

"Really?" Ada thought back over all the hours of listening she'd done, about how much Clara was missing her boyfriend and couldn't bear not seeing him, etc.

"Yeah, well, I'll be starting uni soon, won't we? And to be honest I don't want to be tied down when I get there."

Clara was hoping to go to Birmingham to study history and – unlike Ada, who had decided to delay a year before she began her course – after so many months cooped up with her family, she was keen to get going as soon as possible.

"That's surprisingly sensible for you," Ada said.

"Rude! But anyway, sensible is the last thing I'm intending to be, believe me!"

For some reason, Ada hadn't told Clara about Ben. Well, she knew the reason really, and that was that he'd asked her not to tell anyone. He was scared about losing his job, she realised that, but she would have dearly loved to share her news with her friend. To have Clara listen to her for a change.

"But you might be disappointed," Ada cautioned. "I don't think Freshers' week will be what it was. Everything's online. And somebody in my art class was saying they'd heard we won't be able to have people to stay overnight, or have parties, or anything like that."

"Don't dampen my spirits!" laughed Clara. "I'm sure we'll find a way to have fun."

"I'm sure," Ada smiled, realising how much she missed her friend. But while Clara had spent much of her social time with James she hadn't questioned what Ada was doing with hers, which was useful really, as it would be hard to out-and-out lie to her.

To celebrate the end of the girls' school years, Louisa had asked if Clara and her family would like to come round to their house, and they could have a mini celebration in the garden. While she loved this idea, Ada was also itching to see Ben as well. There was nothing for it, though. He would have to wait, although she had been glad to see him at college, and she could see from his eyes

– the only features visible above his face mask – that he was smiling at her before he turned hurriedly away.

It was a hot, sunny afternoon and Clara, Ada and Lily played a few games of boules and swingball, while Louisa, Andy and Mary sat and drank prosecco in the shade. Harry had opted not to come.

"I think he needs some space!" Andy had laughed.

"He's not the only one," Clara muttered. But she was happy. She had the grades she needed, and Ada had hers too.

"I can't believe we're going to be so far apart!" Clara had wailed. "Why don't you come to Birmingham?"

"Why don't you come to Sussex? We've got the sea! Anyway, I'm not starting for another year. You'll be a grown-up second-year by then. You won't want to bother with a little fresher like me."

"As if!" Clara said.

"I am going to miss you, though." Ada hugged her friend tightly.

"Together since we were four!" Clara said. "Mum, will you take some pictures of me and Ada?"

"Of course!" Mary smiled, standing up. "Goodness, I feel a bit tipsy!"

"Mum!" Clara rolled her eyes.

"Can't take her anywhere!" said Andy. "Come on, I'll take the photos. Give me your phones!"

"I want some too," said Louisa. "My god, look at you two. All grown up!"

"Mum, are you crying?"

"No," Louisa sniffed. "I've got some grit in my eye."

"Ahh Louisa," Mary said, putting an arm around her. "You have got a soft side!"

"Mary!" Andy said but Louisa just laughed.

"I have," she agreed. "I just don't always show it. Honestly, I remember Ada's first day at primary like it was yesterday, and how she went on and on about this girl called Clara, and now look at them, still together after all these years. And they've done us proud. Congratulations, girls!"

"Yes, well done you two, you're wonderful. We're going to miss you."

At this, Lily started crying.

"Hey," Clara said softly, "what's up, Lil?"

"I don't want you to go! I don't want to be stuck at home with just Mum and Dad."

"Thanks very much," laughed Andy.

"Can I come and visit, Clara?"

"I don't think we're allowed to have guests overnight," said Clara. "Because of Covid." Ada shot her a look. "Maybe one day," she relented.

"And with you, Ada, when you go?"

"Sure, Lily! Of course."

Louisa gave the older girls a glass of prosecco each, and a smaller one to Lily, so that they could all raise a toast. Gradually, the afternoon drifted into the evening, the air tinged with the scent of Louisa's jasmine flowers. They ordered takeaway pizzas and the girls were allowed another glass of wine, and another.

As night fell swiftly, and far earlier than it had just a few weeks ago, Clara and her family got up to leave, and there were kisses and hugs, which were not strictly allowed but – "I bet Boris and Matt Handcock are kissing people," said Andy – sometimes you just had to do what felt right.

When their guests had gone, Louisa and Ada shared a hug and then, mentioning how tired they both felt, they put on the kettle and made cups of tea to take up to their beds, wishing each other goodnight then shutting their bedroom doors and picking up their phones.

Louisa was eager to swap clandestine messages with her new boyfriend, blissfully unaware that in the next room her daughter was doing exactly the same thing.

Ada

During the meal out with Mum and Jude on the first
night, Archie is well-mannered and polite, the epitome
of a nice young man, but he doesn't know Mum's
background with men, or Gran's for that matter. Neither
are big proponents of relationships, and while my
friends were encouraged to have boyfriends round –
sometimes even superseding friendships – my mum
would always remind me that friends come first. Which,
given she's not really somebody who has a lot of friends,
or at least she didn't back then, was an interesting take
for her to have. But she would caution me to learn from
her mistakes – without spelling out what those mistakes
were. And she'd tell me not to let work rule my life, all
the while letting it rule hers. I suppose that might have
been one of the mistakes she meant, and I suppose also
that it's not an easy thing to back out of. Particularly
when you're earning a lot of money and have a nice
house, expensive holidays, and of course expensive cars.

Anyway, all of this meant for Archie that he was not
going to get the easy ride I suspect he might have done
with some girls' parents. Would he impress dads? Would
they find him too confident, too smooth, too good-looking?
I don't know. I'm entirely unfamiliar with the father-
daughter relationship I've heard about, where the father

jokes that he doesn't ever want his daughter to have a boyfriend. Ha ha. Mum says that's just another form of patriarchal ownership. My sociology teacher at sixth form, Miss Rogers, said something similar. The boys said she was a lesbian. She was. But does that make the point any less valid?

Still, while I agree with these things, there is also a part of me that would just like a normal upbringing, where boyfriends are welcomed and at least given a chance, without being judged or – as in Archie's case – pre-judged. Consequently, I am not exactly my most relaxed during the meal, which is up at Tregynon Manor. Archie says all the right things, about the beautiful house and amazing view. He talks about the art there, and the sculptures in the gardens, then about his own work plans, and he talks about me. He says lovely things about how pleased he is we met, and how wonderful my artwork is but I am not able to appreciate this as much as I should. Because I'm looking for Mum's reaction.

Jude is no problem. She is sweet and interested, asking Archie questions about his family and interests. In fact, in many ways Jude is the archetypal 'mum'. She is pleasant and welcoming. My actual mum, being Mum, is… fine. I'm afraid that's really the best I can say. But afterwards, as Archie and I walk back to Gran's (she didn't come out with us, saying she was tired), he seems happy enough and talks about how great Mum and Jude are and how lucky I am, to have an alternative kind of background and a beautiful place to live.

"Do you really think so?"

"Yeah!" he says, turning to me. "This is incredible. Honestly. Your mum's like this amazingly successful businesswoman. Jude's a political whirlwind. Your grandma's ninety-something but she acts like she's about our age. All these strong women in your life, Ada. It's no wonder you're like you are."

"I don't know if that's a compliment!" I laugh.

"Course it is!" he puts his hands on my shoulders. "You're not like other girls."

I think I like that but what does it mean? That he just doesn't see me in 'that way'?

He leans forwards and I wonder if he's going to kiss me but instead he wraps me in a huge hug and says, "I really love you, Ada."

It's very confusing.

We spend the next day in St Ives, visiting all of the art shops and galleries, spending time in the little museum, where we see a stuffed animal that we are told was the world's smallest dog, Tiny.

I can't take my eyes off this little furry four-legged figure, enclosed in a glass dome and described as 'the world's most wonderful dog'.

"It's not real!" Archie says.

"But look at it. What if it is?"

"It's not!" he scoffs and takes my hand to pull me across to an art display. He keeps my hand in his. It feels so good. I don't want him to let go, and he doesn't.

We wander around the museum, taking our time, reading about the different industries in the area and prominent figures and Archie says he loves it here, and I imagine him coming to live in Cornwall, the two of us setting up something arty, spending free time on the beaches, surfing, swimming, walking the coastal path...

And yet, in my heart I know he's too flighty. And even deeper in my heart, I wonder if all of that is really what I want. I don't know. But I do know I want him.

As we exit the museum, he squeezes my hand and lets go. We wander to the busy harbourside and walk along to the lighthouse at the very tip of the harbour. The tide is in and the clean, clear water laps against the old walls.

A couple of girls a bit younger than us are sitting dangling their legs over the side of the harbour. I see Archie's eyes on them and it irritates me; even though I have no right to feel that way.

We find our balance once more as we head back into the town and pick up a couple of freshly baked pasties which we take to the small tropical gardens, where we sit on a bench and eat. Archie snakes his arm along the back of the bench so it's sort of around my shoulders and sort of not. I don't know whether to lean back and I end up sitting slightly uncomfortably, turned to face him as we talk about the different artists whose work we've seen so far.

"Can't believe I've got to go again tomorrow," Archie says, his eyes seeking mine. "I'm going to miss you."

"I'll miss you too," I say. It feels like the time is slipping away and I realise my half-formed hopes of something happening between us really are going to be dashed.

"Can I come back another time, do you think?"

"Of course!" My heart leaps.

"Great. And by then I want you set up with your own gallery and regular exhibitions, OK?"

"So you're not coming back for another twenty years?"

"I think it'll be sooner than that," he smiles, his hand moving onto my shoulder.

Is this it? Could this be the moment he kisses me, I wonder, hastily wiping pasty crumbs off my hand and wishing I didn't have the taste of cheese and onion in my mouth.

Archie's hand begins to massage my neck, gently. "You're very tense," he says.

"Not very."

"Well you don't feel quite relaxed." He takes his hand away but stands and moves behind the bench, where he puts both his hands on my shoulders and starts to rub them gently. "Does that feel good?" he asks.

Like you wouldn't believe, I think, but I don't say that.

"Mmm," I say. "That is nice."

"Just nice?" he laughs.

"Really nice," I say. I wonder if I've got dandruff and if so whether he will notice.

"Can I take you out tonight?" he asks. "Just you and me? Do you think your gran would mind?"

"Of course," I say. "I mean, of course you can take me out. I don't think Gran will mind at all."

"Great."

And then he kisses me! Except, it's a kind kiss. Fond. Brotherly, on the top of my head, as he finishes the massage and moves around the side of the bench, eager to be off again. I stand as well, depositing our rubbish in a nearby bin, and we walk down the slope and back along the main street, where Archie decides he needs to buy some clothes, and fudge for his mum, and cider for his sister. Once more, I'm confounded and confused by his feelings and his intentions, but I suppose time will tell.

2020

And then it was September. With it came that familiar back-to-school feeling, as the air became lighter somehow; fresher – even in London – and the sun hung lower in the sky, retiring earlier each day.

It has its own associations, this time of year. More so even than a New Year's Day, September can be a time of promise and new beginnings. Back to school and work, refreshed and invigorated by summer. Resolutions to do well; do better; find success. Shiny new shoes, fresh-from-the-packet shirts, unblemished blazers. Pencil cases packed neatly with their cargo and unsullied exercise books piled neatly in schools, awaiting their new owners.

Except this year, these early September days came and went and Ada watched from the window as mothers passed by with their little offspring, some full of excitement and some full of fear, all neat and tidy in their uniform. Older kids dawdled, eyes glued to phone screens, reluctantly returning to reality.

She turned back to her laptop, scanning job sites for something to help tide her over during her 'gap year'. Ada thought she might want to go travelling at some point and she really didn't want to ask Louisa to pay for it. Part of her wished she'd just gone straight to university, like Clara was doing.

Still, she had her place secured for the following year and for now she was free. It was just that this freedom which she thought she had longed for was actually a bit daunting. And, she feared, it may just turn out to be a very long, very boring year.

Ben, who was back at work, had been encouraging her to take the chance to work on her art. He envied the freedom she had and he hoped that she might change her degree subject from Anthropology and Art History, to something more art-focused. More creative. "From a purely teaching point of view," he'd said, "I'd advise you not to waste your talent. Develop it! Or you'll end up a teacher like me."

"You're a brilliant teacher," she'd told him. "Everyone loves you."

"Thanks," he'd said, but for him it wasn't quite the compliment she'd meant it as. He had once had ambitions, to travel the world and gain inspiration and let his ideas flow; translate them into something wonderful. Instead, he'd got together with Amber, and they'd hatched a plan to be together, which meant him going to university locally, living with his parents and training as a teacher, saving his money while Amber saved hers, so they could get a place to live as soon as they graduated.

They'd made it happen – Amber had made it happen, being a planner and an instigator and incredibly driven. But the last couple of years he had felt like he was dragging his feet, and now he'd met Ada and was torn. When he thought of her going away the following year, he wanted to go with her, be free like her. He sometimes wondered if he could; work this year out at school, end things with Amber and then move to the coast, take a risk for once.

But he didn't have it in him; he couldn't hurt Amber like that, and would Ada even want him to anyway? Realistically, she would change a lot over the next year or two. She would maybe go travelling in a few months' time and no doubt meet some gorgeous, bronzed backpacker called Brad or something. Besides, he was back to teaching properly now. Back in college, with a new tranche of hopeful students looking to him, ready to be inspired. He had planning and marking to do, and a wedding to rearrange.

Ada was lovely. She was beautiful. Talented. Thoughtful. Incredible.

Ada was eighteen.

Ben knew it was time for him to be the grown-up.

Her lovely face fell. He couldn't bear it.

"But I thought you liked me." She inwardly kicked herself for sounding so pathetic.

"But Ada," he said gently, wanting to kiss her but knowing it would be the wrong thing now. That it had been the wrong thing before. "You know we can't carry on like this. It's not right, from so many perspectives. And I know you're not my student anymore, but I could still lose my job over this."

Ada wasn't stupid. She knew he was right, but she loved him. She was sure she did. Yet as she walked away that day, leaving Ben wracked with guilt behind her, Ada thought that dawning somewhere inside her, mingled with sadness, was a slight sense of relief.

Ada

On the way back home, Archie and I stop at Carbis Bay for a swim. It's quieter here than it was in St Ives and the weather is wonderful, the skies open and blue, and the sea is as calm as it ever is.

"I love the way it changes here," I say as we bob up and down, treading water. "This can be the most dramatic, scariest place in the world when the weather's bad. I wouldn't set foot in the sea some days, maybe not even on the beach. And then there are days like today, when everything's…"

"Perfect?"

"Yes," I say, and I look at him, his skin glistening as it had that day in Josh's lake. Does Archie remember it too? Did it even mean anything to him? I suppose he has come all this way to see me. He must feel something for me, or why make all this effort?

I am so aware of his proximity, and the fact that we are both in essentially just our underwear.

But then he bobs under the water and he comes up again a few metres away, laughing. "I love the sea!" he shouts.

"Me too!" I laugh and do the same as him. Even with my eyes closed, the saltwater stings them a little, but it feels so good. I feel so alive.

"Come on," I call, and I front-crawl through the gentle waves, parallel to the beach. He follows suit. He's a good swimmer but I know I'm faster. For once, I have the upper hand. I slow down and wait for him. "Keep up!"

Something about that moment is the catalyst. He reaches out for me. "Like that, is it?" he asks, and he pulls me towards him, and then he's kissing me. And it is exactly as good as I've imagined. Better, even, here under the benevolent gaze of the sun and both of us held in the embrace of the sea. I hear the voices of children playing further along the shore, and a dog barking somewhere; the gulls crying overhead and the softest whisper of the waves. I don't want the moment to end.

But end it must. Still, Archie is reluctant as he pulls away. "Wow."

"Wow," I agree.

"Should we find somewhere a bit more private?" he asks.

"I would love to. But I don't know where."

"Will your mum be in? Could we go to your room at her place?" His arms are around my waist.

"I don't know about that," I say. The thought makes me uncomfortable.

"I could sneak you into my room at your gran's!" he laughs but I suspect he is only half joking. Again, I feel uneasy.

"Argh!" he exclaims. "There must be somewhere!"

I kiss him gently. "It'll work itself out. Maybe Gran will be out when we get back." I doubt it somehow, and to be honest even if she was I don't think I'd be able to relax enough.

"We could look for somewhere secluded on the way back…" he grins.

"Well, let's keep an eye out." I don't necessarily mean it but then again I could be persuaded to lose myself in the moment with Archie.

Come on Ada, I tell myself, *this is what you've wanted to happen for ages. And you're young, and free, and you're in control of your own life.*

I kiss him again and he willingly returns the kiss, running the tips of his fingers up my spine so that I shiver.

"OK," I say, "let's see if we can find somewhere."

We dry off on the beach, looking slightly shyly at each other and hopping into our clothes despite still wearing our wet swimwear. We sit on our towels in the car and I know I'll have to give the seats a clean and a hoover; leaving sand and seawater in Mum's pride and joy is a no-no. But that is not for now. I start the engine and think through our options.

"I know somewhere," I say, and Archie grins, putting his hand on my knee.

I take a deep, slow breath. I need to focus on driving, not that hand. We head off and up one of the back roads, which takes us away from the sea, into the part of this place less inhabited by people and tourists. I pull up at a layby and we climb out, Archie kissing me again, pushing me gently against the car.

I feel like I will remember this moment forever; the quiet of this place broken only by the cries of a pair of buzzards high overhead; the heat of the sun and the thin layer of sand on my skin crunching lightly against the car as Archie presses against me, his hand travelling to my thigh.

"Not here!" I whisper, smiling at him. "Come on."

We climb a stile and I take him away, off the beaten

path, through scratchy undergrowth, till we reach a little outcrop of stones.

"What is this place?" he asks, his hand creeping under the strap of my top and stroking my back.

"I think it's some kind of ancient monument, but the landowner's not keen on people coming up here so they've let it get overgrown. My uncle showed me how to get here."

Laurie had taken me and Mum on a walk the Christmas we'd all been together at Gran's, and we'd walked to this place. It had not been as overgrown then, the shrubbery having died back in the winter, and we'd sat on the stones and drunk coffee from a flask as the wind blew around us. It was grey and bleak then, whereas today is bright, and still, and hot.

Archie kisses me and I allow myself to just focus on him, and his mouth on mine, and his hands on me, and we're slowly moving against the rock and down to the ground, where he places his hoodie beneath me and kisses me tenderly, and I can see the sky above me, and feel his hot breath on me, and I think this might be the most perfect day ever.

We rest a while afterwards, pleased with ourselves and enjoying the shade of the rocks against the sun. Then I hear voices and I peer up and across the top of the gorse. I see a group of walkers crossing the stile. They will almost certainly be sticking to the path but they also might know this place.

"We need to make ourselves respectable," I say, which makes Archie laugh. Staying low down, we pull clothes back on and into place.

Archie kisses me again. "That was amazing."

"It was." I smile. Checking my watch, I say, "Maybe we should get going. Then we can spend a bit of time with Gran before we go out."

"Oh, yeah, erm, about that…"

I look at him but I don't say anything.

"I don't know if I can afford it, Ada. I need to save my money for the flat deposit really. London is really expensive, you know."

I do know, I think. *I'm from London. I grew up there.*

His manner strikes me suddenly as slightly condescending. But I just say, "Oh, OK, that's not a problem. We can just have tea with Gran. Maybe get something on the way back?"

"Well erm, I was actually thinking maybe I should head off this evening you know."

Now my heart sinks. "Really?"

"Yeah, sorry Ada. I feel like a bit of a shit really."

"Oh?"

"I'm kind of seeing somebody at home, someone I went to school with, and she messaged earlier. I hadn't told her I was visiting, you know, a girl, but she's found out. I just feel a bit bad about, you know, all this…"

I am actually lost for words. I turn and walk away from him.

"Ada!" he says and tries to take my hand but I shake him off.

The group of walkers are going the other way, I see, and I'm glad because I don't want them to see me with these hot, angry tears of humiliation on my face.

"I do really like you," he says.

"Fuck off, Archie."

"Fair enough," he says. And I'm annoyed that he doesn't fight harder, but at the same time I know it would be utterly meaningless if he did.

We walk in silence to the car and I get in then open his door for him.

"We'll go back and you can get your bag and walk to the station," I say. "It's not far. In fact, when we get back you don't go in, OK? I'll get your bag and you can go."

"OK," he says quietly. I can't even look at him. I don't know if I am more angry with him or with myself.

I park the car at Mum's and send her a message apologising for the sand on the seats and promising to clear it up.

Don't worry, she sends straight back. **Hope you're having a good day xx**

That makes me feel even worse.

Archie trails behind me and once we get to Godolphin Terrace, I tell him to wait. "I'll go and get your stuff."

"Can I just use the loo?" he asks.

"No." I storm off along the street but I am quiet entering Gran's house. Thankfully she must be having her siesta so I can creep up the stairs, throw Archie's stuff into his bag and leave again without seeing her.

"Here you go," I say, thrusting the bag at Archie's chest.

"Thanks," he says. "Ada, I'm really sorry."

"OK. See you."

I turn and stomp back down the street, not looking back. I am sad but not heartbroken and there's a little part of me that is proud of myself for giving him his marching orders, even if it is too little too late.

2020

"You don't mind do you, Ada? I am sorry," Louisa said.

"No not at all, Mum." She really didn't. They'd had tickets to go to the local cinema but when Louisa told her that she had to go out for a work 'thing', Ada really didn't mind at all. "To be honest I'll be tired after work, anyway. I'll probably just have a bath, maybe get a takeaway, and have an early night."

It felt a little disingenuous (because it was), but Ada had something very different in mind.

She scrolled through her phone conversations.

Hi again, she sent. **I'm alone tomorrow evening. Want to come over?**

She waited, drumming her fingers nervously.

Ping.

To your place?

Yes. Where else? A newly independent working woman – she had managed to get a long-term temp job at a film production company – she felt emboldened.

I don't know... what about your mum?

She's out all night. And we won't be seen if you come over here.

More finger-drumming.

OK. I'll be there at eight. Just let me know if anything changes.

At 7.58, the doorbell went. Ada pretended that she had not been sitting on the bottom step nervously.

"Hello," she said, in her best, most grown-up voice.

"Hi," Ben said, and he followed her into the dark hallway, and they stopped and looked at each other in the dim light that fell from the lounge, laughing in their happiness to see each other, and then his face turned serious, and then they were kissing each other.

Despite all best intentions, Ben had found himself drawn back to Ada. He'd felt better once he'd ended things and could almost convince himself nothing had happened. Not really. And it was probably just the stress of Covid and lockdowns, and the forthcoming wedding. In this way, he let himself off the hook. He had a new intake of students to get to work with, who seemed younger than ever.

Work kept him busy and he did his best to get involved in the wedding planning, except he could tell that his input only irritated Amber and so he left her to it. Then, one Sunday when she'd gone to a wedding fair with her best mate Beth, he'd heard his phone ping. And there was that familiar name, which he'd tried so hard to forget.

Ada Morgan.

Shit. What should he do? Just ignore it?

Hi Ben, her message began. **Sorry to bother you but I wondered if you would be my reference for this job I've applied for? I wouldn't ask but I don't have any previous employers and they want to hear from somebody who can vouch for my character.**

Bloody hell. Couldn't she have asked one of her other teachers?

Sure, he sent back. **Just let me know who to contact and what you need me to say.**

Thank you so much. I'll email you the form they've sent me.

And that was that. There were no kisses, no mention of missing him or wishing things were different. Ben breathed a sigh of relief and opened his email.

***

On her side of this exchange, Ada had been fretting for nearly two days over whether or not to ask him. Of course, she could have asked Miss Rogers, but she didn't have any direct contact details for her and besides, Miss Rogers didn't know her as well as Ben did. And Ada really wanted this job. She knew he'd say good things about her.

As she had composed the first message, Ada's palms were sweaty and as she pressed 'send' she had butterflies in her tummy – *not literally*, she remembered Louisa's words to her on that first day at primary school.

But she kept her messages brief and polite. For one thing, Amber could have been sitting right next to him.

Despite this, when he messaged straight back she couldn't help hoping that he'd say how much he was missing her, and beg her to come back. The matter-of-fact reply was disappointing.

So she thanked him, and promised to send him the form by email. She duly did, and he filled it in, sending it straight to her soon-to-be employer. Then he thought again and forwarded the form to Ada so she could see what he said.

Ada was an outstanding student with a great deal of talent. She handed in work to a very high standard, always on time. She was a popular member of the class and a pleasure to teach.

Thank you so much! X

She sent a quick WhatsApp to him and couldn't help adding that kiss. It struck the chord she wanted but this wasn't mirrored in Ben's reply.

No problem. It's all true.

And that was that, or so Ada thought. Yes, she was disappointed, but what had she expected, really? Ben had ended things with her, and he was right to do so. But he liked her. She knew he did. And she was lonely, with Clara and many of her other friends gone to uni.

Starting work was nerve-racking too, although it was a lovely small office and the people were very friendly.

They were just quite a bit older than her, and although it was in a creative industry, her role was far from inspired. Opening and sorting mail, setting up an electronic filing system, typing correspondence; even doing the drinks run to a local coffee shop. But it was a job, and experience, and money, she reminded herself. Nevertheless, as she sat on a bench one lunchtime, eating the salad she'd brought from home, she was thrilled to see Ben's name appear on her phone.

So did you get the job?

He had not been able to help himself, as Ada insisted on popping into his head. Memories of the summer meetings they'd enjoyed. Those kisses they'd shared… Surely it wouldn't hurt just to check in on how she was doing.

Yes. Thank you. I'm on my lunch break at the moment.

That's great! I'm on my lunch too. What are you having?

So began a conversation between them, and in this banal way their relationship resumed, quickly accelerating from questions about lunch to discussions about how each of them was feeling, about work and about life. Both were lonely in their own way.

And now here he was, in her house. It was such a relief to see her again.

"In here," she said, leading him into the lounge.

"We can't. What if your mum comes back?"

"She won't."

"She might. Where's your room?"

So she led him by the hand, up the stairs, both of them giggling in the quiet house, and they kissed in the darkness of her bedroom, the open curtains letting in the lights from the street. And they fell onto her bed, a hundred glow-in-the-dark stars looking down on them, all thoughts of mums and fiancées banished.

***

Afterwards, they lay in each other's arms and, despite their best intentions, fell asleep. Ada woke with a shock to see it was nearly eleven. She checked her phone for a message from Louisa but there was nothing so presumably she was still out. Ada certainly hoped so.

Waking Ben gently, she kissed him. "Time to get up."

Ben smiled and pulled her to him.

"We can't," Ada said. "Mum will be back soon."

They held each other tightly, and Ada felt Ben shiver slightly against her.

She pulled away slightly. "Are you crying?" she asked, surprised.

"No. Not really."

"Because of Amber?"

"Partly. And because of you. And..."

"It's wrong, isn't it?" Ada asked.

"I suppose it is. But it doesn't feel wrong."

"Amber would be upset."

"She'd be devastated." He laughed roughly and without humour. "God, I..."

"Wait!" Ada said, putting her finger to her lips. "What?"

"Ssh..." She wrapped a sheet around herself and tiptoed to the window. "It's Mum!" she hissed. "And she's... with somebody. They're kissing. Shit."

"Do you know him?" Ben asked.

"No, I... don't worry about that. You need to get out of here, now."

He didn't need telling twice, and started pulling on his clothes, carrying his shoes down the stairs as they tiptoed to the back door. Ada kissed him quickly, then let him out, locking the door behind her and running back upstairs.

She was out of breath as she reached her window and breathed a sigh of relief to see her mum and the man were talking and, oh, now they were kissing again...

Ada got into bed and under the covers, only now allowing herself to think over the evening. Perhaps it was best they'd had to cut things short, and not had time for a long, protracted goodbye. But she wished Ben could have stayed all night. And she wondered where he was now; could he have got out of the back gate? Was he tucked into the bushes somewhere, waiting to exit via the front? She pictured him tiptoeing round, and maybe that man her mum was with seeing him. Wat if they thought he was a burglar, or worse? There was nothing she could do about it now.

Ada realised she was holding her breath at the thought of it all. She exhaled slowly and heard her mum's key in the lock, then footsteps on the stairs.

Slow it down, Ada, she told herself.

Louisa, feeling a bit guilty for being out so late on an evening she was meant to have spent with her daughter, and worried that Ada may have seen her with AJ, was relieved to reach her bedroom and look in to find that Ada was tucked up in bed and fast asleep. She stood for a moment and admired her beautiful girl, marvelling at her youth and innocence.

Ada

In times of anguish growing up, my first port of call has always been Clara. While she and I are still pretty much as close as ever, and she will always be my best friend – she is practically a sister to me – she's not such an immediate part of my life at the moment as she used to be. Besides, she doesn't know all my uni friends, and I don't know hers.

Over the last three years, Josh has become almost as vital to me as Clara and I feel bad that I have been a bit slack at keeping in touch with him since I've been in Cornwall. Still, I know I can count on him now for a sympathetic ear.

"Am I meant to be surprised?"

I've just told Josh everything that's happened with Archie. This is not the response I expected.

"What do you mean?"

"Well, it's Archie, isn't it? I mean – and don't take this the wrong way – Archie wants to sleep with everyone."

His words register with a dull thump.

"Thanks very much."

"Ada," he sighs. "I don't mean he doesn't like you. He's fancied you since first year."

"Really?" Pathetically, my hopes are lifted a little by this but really it's like raising a wet sock up a flagpole.

"Yes, really. But – reality check – he also fancied Sasha

and Pippa and Charlotte (don't tell Will about that), and the girl at the café in the union, and Dr Alice Roberts, and Taylor Swift…"

I can hear a slight note of amusement in Josh's voice but there is also kindness there.

"OK, OK, I get what you're saying."

"Ada my lovely friend, you know what he's like. I don't think this is a surprise to you really, is it?"

"No," I admit. "I suppose not."

"Did you have a good time with him?"

"Yes, until…"

"Forget that bit. Did you have a good time? Was he nice to your mum, and Elise, and Jude?"

"Yes, I think perhaps even Mum liked him a little bit."

Josh laughs. "I'm really sorry to say it but I think you've probably had the best you're going to get from Archie. At least till he turns thirty and decides it's time to settle down, but I'm not convinced that's going to happen even then."

And so that's that. I know Josh is right really. While I had hoped for a little more sympathy, I'm grateful for his honesty, and realism. There's no point offering worthless platitudes, and false hope. Josh is, as always, being the best kind of friend.

"Anyway," he says, "I'm planning to come and visit soon too. Not because I think you're going to sleep with me–" we both laugh at this – "but I do miss you."

"I miss you too," I say.

"And besides, Ada Morgan, we've got plans to make. I can't have you languishing away and neglecting your sizeable talents."

"I don't know about that," I laugh.

It's funny, how at uni I'd felt like I could do it; I could make a living, or at least a partial living, from my art, but since I've been here I've begun to think I was living in a dream world. A lovely little bubble, where my friends and I lived and worked and played, and discussed all manner of things, thinking we had it all weighed up and were going to change the world. Now that the bubble has burst and I'm back to living with my mum, and following her rules, I have allowed doubt to creep in. Who really makes a living from art? Maybe Archie's got the right idea, using his skills and talent in a more commercial way.

"Well, I know," Josh says firmly. "Now, what are you doing the weekend after next?"

"Erm... not a lot. I think I've got a shift on the Saturday but I'm off on the Sunday." The lifeguarding is keeping me afloat – no pun intended – financially, and although I don't feel quite a part of the team yet, it is nice to have some company my age or thereabouts. When I think back to my gap year temping in that office, I know I am so much better off working outside and not stuck at a desk all day.

"Perfect. I'm coming to Cornwall. But don't worry about putting me up. I'm actually bringing Granny with me. We're staying at the posh hotel on the cliffs."

"Tregynon?"

"That's the one. Granny says she knows it from her childhood."

"Really?"

"Yes, not sure how. But she's keen to get over to Cornwall, she says, while she still can. She's a bit doddery these days."

"Yeah, Gran's not doing quite so well either."

"It's horrible, isn't it?"

"I hate it," I admit. I think of my amazing grandmother, and how she's always been so fit and strong, to the point that you would struggle to put an age to her. Now, it seems all of a sudden it's really beginning to show. And I don't think she goes on those night-time walks she used to do.

She doesn't know I know about them, but one summer when Clara and I stayed with Gran, we saw her going out one night and I was a bit worried – as well as a little intrigued – so we followed her, at a distance, keeping to the shadows.

"What if she's running a smuggling ring?" Clara whispered, and we both collapsed in giggles, and Gran's head turned slightly but she didn't see us, or recognise us at least. She probably just assumed we were a couple of girls heading home after a few drinks.

We waited a moment before following her again and then we stayed in the shadow of some trees, up the slope from the beach where she wandered along the sand, stopping every now and then to look out across the sea, before turning back and heading in the direction of Godolphin Terrace.

We turned and ran, managing to get home some time before her and galloping up the stairs. When we heard the front door open we had to try really hard not to giggle and give ourselves away. We listened to Gran go into the kitchen and make herself a drink, and then she tiptoed quietly up the stairs, obviously thinking we were fast asleep. When she shut her bedroom door behind her, we relaxed, and looked at each other.

"Your gran's a legend!" Clara whispered.

"I know!" I felt really proud of Gran, although I knew that my mum wouldn't approve of her going out on her own at night.

Ever since then, when I stayed with Gran I'd keep an ear out for her leaving and returning late at night, but the last time I was here I don't think she did it once. It seems that she's letting her age begin to wash over her these days, like the tide creeping in across the sand.

After my phone call with Josh, I go downstairs to find Gran, who's in the kitchen rooting through her fridge.

"No Alfie?" she asks. She has continued calling him this, knowing full well what his actual name is.

"No, he... had to go," I say. "What are you looking for?"

"The butter," she says.

I gently take the butter from her hand and hold it up.

"Oh my!" she laughs. "I must have taken it out of the fridge so I could look for it. I think I'm finally losing my marbles, Ada. It had to happen sometime."

"I'm sure you're not, Gran," I say. It makes me feel uncomfortable to hear her talking like that. "I do that kind of thing all the time."

"Well, you're never too young to lose your marbles!" She laughs and I do too. "Anyway, what's all this about your young man leaving so soon?"

"He's not my young man," I say. "I think he might be somebody else's."

"I get the feeling he might be one of those who's not anyone's really, my love," she says, looking at me as if trying to read my feelings. "He wouldn't be the first. Do you want to tell me about it?"

"There's not much to tell really," I say.

"Well, that's fine. Let's just sit and have a cuppa shall we, and see what comes out?"

"Alright," I say. "Thank you, Gran."

The toaster chooses that moment to eject its load.

"Oh yes, I was making some toast, too! Would you like some?" Gran asks.

The thought of hot buttered toast and a cup of tea sitting in Gran's cosy front room suddenly seems like the most enticing thing in the world. "That would be lovely, thank you. Can I make it, though?"

"No, no, you go and sit down. Let me look after you. I want to."

Those words are almost enough to bring me to tears. I do as I'm told and I go through and sit on Gran's sofa, tucking my legs up onto the seat and holding one of her cushions on my lap. I listen to her busying herself in the kitchen and I look around me, thinking of her life here.

When she moved to this house, it belonged to her old English teacher, who had been a friend of Gran's mum, Annabel. Annabel died while Gran was at school here in Cornwall and when the war was over and Gran completed her education, Angela Forbes took her in.

I try to picture what life was like then, and how it has changed. There would have been no TV, of course. No radiators and central heating.

I imagine cosy evenings in front of the fire, perhaps listening to the radio (the wireless, Gran would say) or just the sound of the flames fighting each other for their share of the coal or the wood and whatever else was being burned; a winter wind straight in from the sea howling outside, crying to be let in.

How strange it is to think just how much life and the world have changed during the time that Gran has lived in this one little house. I am so proud of her, and how she's taken it all in her stride. She's old in years but not in attitude. Maybe I will tell her about Archie. Well, perhaps not everything.

"Here we are," she says, placing a tray on the table in front of us. It holds a teapot, a jug of milk, two cups and saucers, and a full toast rack.

"I don't believe it," she laughs. "I've forgotten the butter."

"I'll get it," I say.

"No, I told you, I'm looking after you," she says firmly. "You stay put."

I watch her move back to the kitchen and she returns with the butter, two knives, and two small plates.

"There," she says. "Now we have everything we need."

She sits next to me so that she can pour the tea. Without looking at me, she says, "So what happened?"

"Oh, it's stupid really," I say.

"I'm sure it's not."

"It is, a bit. Honestly. I know what Archie's like. It's obvious, isn't it? I mean, you just have to look at him."

"He's very good looking," Gran admits.

"He is. And he knows it. But he's not vain. Just…"

"Full of himself?" Gran suggests.

"I suppose he is, a bit."

"But I don't mean he's not a nice boy," she says. "You really like him?"

"Yes," I say but even as I say it I wonder, do I really? I mean, the attraction is there, of course. And he is funny and good company, but would I really want him for a boyfriend? In my heart of hearts, I think not.

How could I ever relax in a relationship with him? As Josh correctly said, Archie fancies half the girls he meets. To be fair, he's never tried to hide that about himself. I think of his comment about the girl in the ice-cream shop.

I'm annoyed at him for not telling me he was seeing somebody, but it's worse for his girlfriend than for me. I suppose deep down I'm more annoyed at myself.

"Davey was very good looking," Gran says.

"Grandad?" I say, trying the name out. It sounds strange; too familiar, said about somebody I didn't know and about whom I know very little. He died when Mum was a toddler and what little I do know of him was that he wasn't a great husband to Gran.

"Yes," she says. "Your grandad. He was the best-looking boy in town."

"Really?" I ask.

"Really. And it didn't count for anything, Ada. I can tell you a bit about him if you like, but how much do you want to know?"

"You can tell me anything, Gran."

"I suppose I can. Your generation know much more about life than we did when we were your age. You probably know more about things than I do now. It's the way of the world."

"I don't know, I'm sure we all just know different things depending on our experience."

"Perhaps. Well, I'd like to tell you about my life, if it isn't too boring for you."

"Gran," I say, reaching forward for a slice of toast and the butter knife, "of course it's not. I'd love to know."

And so she begins, starting at the point of leaving school – when she moved in here with Miss Forbes and took up work at Tregynon Manor.

"That must have been strange, going back to work at the place where you'd been living and going to all your lessons and everything."

"It was; it was very odd, really. I don't know which family member's room we'd had as our dorm, me and Violet, but all of a sudden it was out of bounds. I was only allowed upstairs once or twice."

"Were you? What for?"

"Ah well, it was a bit sneaky really, behind her ladyship's back. I got soaked to the skin once, coming to work, and so Mrs Peters – that was the housekeeper – helped me find something of her ladyship's to wear. And again when I took the children to the beach. They've got their own little beach at Tregynon, you know."

"Really?"

"Yes. It's just for the hotel guests now of course. Then, it was just for the family."

"But they let you use it?" I wonder if Gran's just trying to distract me from my woes, by telling me all this. It might actually be working.

"Well, yes, once or twice. The first time was actually with the children and their father."

"Lord...?"

"Lord Camelford-Bassett," she says.

"Wasn't that a bit strange?"

"Yes, it was, I suppose, and I did think so at the time, but it was a lovely afternoon." Her eyes are shining as she thinks back to it. "I took Tabitha into the sea. She was only little, and she was a bit nervous so she clung onto me like a limpet." Gran chuckles. "Then she stayed with her dad on the beach and I went out a bit further with the boys. They were good swimmers, those boys. Good boys, really. And Tabitha was so lovely."

"What happened to them?"

"I actually don't know." Her smile falters. It's as though a cloud has drifted in front of the sun.

I remember her telling me she didn't keep in touch with the family. "Did you work with them for long?"

"No, not really." She pauses, as if trying to decide something. "I... well, it was something and nothing really, but back then it seemed like everything."

"What?" I ask, taking a bite of my toast.

"Something happened."

"What?" I ask again, eager for information now.

"Perhaps he was a bit like your Alfie," Gran says.

"Who? Not Lord..."

"Yes, his lordship. He... well, he kissed me."

"No!" I am sitting forward. This feels like an afternoon with Sasha and the others, filling each other in on any gossip, or romantic (or otherwise) developments.

"Yes!" she laughs. "My goodness, it seems a lifetime ago. It could have been quite a scandal..."

I can scarcely believe what she tells me, about having to go and act as 'ladies maid' for Lady Camelford-Bassett, at some society weekend, and how his lordship made a move on her in the garden one evening.

"It was awful!" she says. "Not the kiss. I quite liked that, to be honest." She looks at me with a smile again, and I feel like I can see the young Elise Morgan shining through. "But there were some of the other so-called gentlemen nearby, and they saw what happened, and

170

they laughed at us. I think that was the worst thing, that they laughed. I ran off, of course, and I was sure I'd be humiliated and sacked, and the talk of the town, but somehow he must have fixed it that I was allowed an escape route. I had to be driven home that night, but the story was that I had an ill relative to attend to. So it got me off the hook, so to speak, but I couldn't go back. I couldn't even say my goodbyes to the children. I was very attached to them, maybe especially Tabitha. I suppose I'd lost all my friends when they left Cornwall after the war, and I'd lost my mum, and all I had except for Angela Forbes was those children."

"Wow," I say. "This is like something out of Jane Austen." My mind has returned to the weekend at Josh's and the memory of Archie in the lake, intermingling with the image of Colin Firth playing Mr Darcy in that famous scene, his white shirt clinging to him.

"Maybe. But I suspect it was something that happened all the time. Always has, maybe always will, but perhaps your generation will do things differently, Ada."

"Maybe," I say. I think of how I reacted to Archie's news this afternoon and how I didn't break down in tears but instead told him where to go.

"I think so. Listen, my love, you will do what is right for you in life, I'm sure, and you'll make up your own mind, but if I could give you any advice it would be that you don't have to settle down in a relationship – not unless it's the right one. Maybe some of them are right for a while. Maybe some are right forever. Lovely Fred and Maudie were meant to be together, I am quite sure of that. But some relationships are wrong from the outset. When I was your age, that wasn't deemed important. The focus was on getting married, having a steady home, having children. All important things, and maybe they were necessary then. Women didn't often earn a full wage, and it was the way the world worked. But it meant there was many a couple unhappy with each other."

"Were you and Grandad unhappy?" I ask.

"I'm sad to say we were. I think... well, he was an unhappy man, I'm afraid. He'd had an unhappy childhood, and it sometimes felt like he just wanted to spread that unhappiness around. So despite his good looks, and his ability to charm, he was not a good husband. He was not a nice dad."

"Really?" I think of Mum and Uncle Laurie.

"Really. Louisa wasn't old enough to know much about it at the time, but Laurie certainly was, and I would say it's affected the way he's lived his life. I used to think I wanted him to meet somebody and settle down but I've had a lot of time to think – a lot –" she chuckles – "and he's been very sensible. He's followed his love of the natural world and he's passionate about it. I used to wonder if he was lonely, and maybe sometimes he is, but he's never told me that."

I think of my lovely uncle, who I must admit I've sometimes considered a bit of an oddball. He's tall and unkempt and he lives on some island off the coast of Scotland, working as a wildlife warden up there. He and Mum could not be more different. But both of them, I realise, have remained single almost all their lives. Is that the effect of their parents' unhappy marriage?

"Over the years, I've come round to a different way of thinking," Gran continues, "and I've got your mum and your uncle to thank for that. Louisa used to almost scare me, she was so driven and single-minded. I was sure I'd never have grandchildren, but then you came along. And look at you, Ada. Look what a beautiful person your mum has brought up. Not that she gets all the credit – most of that lies with you. I feel like the luckiest woman alive sometimes, having you and Lou and Laurie in my life."

"And does it bother you – Mum and Jude?" I ask.

"Bother me? No, why should it? She's good for your mum, is Jude. Does it bother you?"

"No, not really. But it's a bit strange, how everything's shifted. I don't feel quite like I've got a home," I admit. "But that's not because of Jude."

"I can imagine it's been hard. You must miss London."

"I do. I miss my life there, and knowing exactly where I am, and having friends. But now I miss uni too and my friends from there. I suppose I just need to make more of an effort to get to know people here."

"You will," Gran says. "I'm sure of it. If you decide to stay here, you'll find a way in."

"I hope so."

"You have great things ahead of you, Ada."

"That's what Archie said."

"Perhaps he's not a total moron then."

I laugh but I feel a bit of that unhappiness rubbing at me again.

"Listen my lovely," Gran says, finally spreading some butter on a now cool piece of toast, "you have a home here with me, whenever you need it. I do not wish to take you away from your mum and I know how much she's missed you and how happy she is that you are here. But you're welcome to stay with me whenever you want to, and for as long as you like. And you know what you must do when you're here?"

"What?"

"Get up into that attic and get to work. Don't let your creativity dry up. You've got great things ahead of you, remember?"

I think of the attic and all my paints and sketchbooks up there, and suddenly I can think of nowhere else I'd rather be.

2021

Just as people had begun to relax, and rejoice in family Christmases and New Year celebrations, reuniting with people they had only been able to see via Zoom calls, a new lockdown was put into place at the very start of the new year; an attempt to outfox the coronavirus, which was still wreaking havoc across the world.

It was getting tiresome now, the novelty value having long since worn away. Still, Ada was content to stay at home with Louisa. It meant not working, and not getting paid as she'd only been temping, but she didn't miss the work, and she had the luxury of knowing she had a roof over her head; central heating and hot water, electricity and broadband... everything she needed paid for by her mum. And although not earning meant she was unlikely to do any travelling later in the year, she found she didn't really seem to mind. She was suddenly, sometimes painfully, aware that she would not have this time at home with her mum for much longer.

It had been just her and Louisa for Christmas; they had invited Elise but they already knew what her answer would be, even though Louisa had said she'd drive to Cornwall to pick Elise up so that she could avoid any public transport.

Ada was impressed by this offer; she often thought her mum could spend more time with her gran and make a greater effort for her. Yes, Louisa had an incredibly busy life and relentless job, but Ada was very aware that life might be lonely for her gran, with both her son and daughter so many miles away.

It had become even more apparent during the lockdowns, when Elise was literally alone day in, day out. She never, ever complained but it must have been incredibly difficult.

Perhaps, thought Ada, the extremes of the last few months had been enough to make Louisa see that her mum needed her, and stop taking her for granted. Elise wouldn't be around forever, Ada wanted to say, but didn't quite dare.

It was the elderly and those with underlying health conditions who were bearing the brunt of the pandemic. It scared Ada that her gran might be one of these people, and that she wouldn't have had a chance to see her. Who would look after Elise, if she became ill? It was an awful thought and she pushed it away.

Better to focus on the positives, which included this new, softer side to Louisa. Ada thought it must be something to do with that man she'd seen her kissing. But Louisa never let on about him.

As for Ada's own love life, after she and Ben had slept together it was like that very act had made the scales fall from their eyes. For Ada, she suddenly felt scared, by the grown-upness of the situation. Before, it had felt a bit unreal, like they were playing. Now, she saw it for what it was; an affair with a (nearly) married man, and not just any man but one who had been her teacher.

Ben was clearly worried about his relationship but also for his job, although Ada knew she would never let on to anyone about what had happened between them.

She had actually been relieved when Ben called her one day and she could tell from the tone of his voice what he was going to say. He had clearly rehearsed what he had to say and it was pretty much what he'd said to her the first time he'd tried to end things. "I'm so sorry, Ada, but we have to end it, properly. It's... it's not fair to you, and it's not fair to Amber."

Ada had remained quiet, which Ben had taken as a sign that she was heartbroken.

"I know you must be upset," he said, "and I feel awful. I should never have allowed this to happen. I'm meant to be the adult, the responsible one."

Ada was struck suddenly by an image of him hiding in the bushes of their garden while her mum and her supposedly secret man kissed by the gate. She began to giggle.

"You're... you're laughing?" He sounded hurt.

"Yes, I'm... I – sorry."

"It's OK," he said, telling himself maybe it was a lucky escape. She was clearly very immature. Well, he'd learned his lesson. "So, I'd better go."

"OK!" she gasped, through more suppressed laughter. "Bye!"

Ben ended the call, perplexed, his ego bent out of shape, while Ada, in her childhood bedroom; on the very bed where she had slept with him, twinkling fairy lights entwined with her bedframe and casting a soft, magical glow amidst the gloom of the November day, let her laughter subside. She clutched a pillow to her stomach, hugging it tightly, feeling bad for Ben that she had laughed, and worse for Amber, that her fiancé had cheated on her.

And Ada felt stupid, that she'd let herself be drawn into such a clichéd situation. Ben was a bit pathetic, she decided, and she wished she'd never slept with him. But she knew some other people treated sex like it was absolutely nothing; something they could and should do if and when they wanted to, with whomever they wanted. It was no big deal to them and she thought perhaps she should try to be more like that herself.

One of the best things about the new lockdown was that Clara was back home, although Clara herself didn't necessarily see this as a good thing. Still, she was delighted to be back with her best friend, and she and Ada could meet up for walks, which they did, every day, even in the rain, wrapping up in thick coats and hats and gloves, pulling hoods back so they could hear each other during the inevitable downpours. Sometimes they'd strike it lucky and enjoy a crisp, cold, blue-skied day, but usually it was at best dull. The world felt subdued. Unable to go about their normal lives, these daily walks with each other helped to keep them on an even keel.

It was easy to pick their friendship straight back up. Clara was glad to be away from her flatmates, who she wasn't all that keen on, although she said that she had started to get to know some of the people on her course and they were talking about sharing a house the following year. Ada tried not to feel jealous of these new people in her friend's life.

Clara also had a new boyfriend, and Ada couldn't help thinking how Clara didn't seem able to be single for long. There was a part of Ada that would have loved to shock her friend by telling her about Ben. Any benefit from that would be short-lived though, and although she didn't think Clara would tell anyone else, it wasn't worth risking anything, for Ben's sake.

"Shall we go to Cornwall this summer?" Ada asked. She had missed their annual holiday the previous year.

"Yes!" Clara exclaimed. "Of course. We're doing that every year for the rest of our lives."

Ada laughed, pleased. She had half-feared that Clara would be intending to go on holiday with her boyfriend instead. She slipped her arm through her friend's, which wasn't really in line with social distancing, but so be it.

"I've missed you."

"I've missed you, too."

"Friends first?"

"Always."

Ada

"Josh!" I call out, even more excited to see him than I thought I would be. Just seeing his face makes me quicken my pace along the platform. His grandmother had apparently insisted on coming by train and I can't say I blame her. The journey does provide some spectacular views.

She wants to talk as well, Josh had messaged me. **About 'the future'.**

Sounds intriguing?

Sounds worrying. Maybe I really am about to be sent off into the C of E.

Would that make you Father Josh? I like it.

It does have a certain ring to it. Maybe...

During this exchange it occurred to me that if it weren't for Josh's complete lack of religious belief, life as a vicar might not sit too badly with him. He's a kind, thoughtful and socially aware person; a great listener and somebody who likes to take action on things.

I hug my friend and I look for his grandmother, who can only be the small, smiling older woman behind him. Stepping back from my hug, I look to her and Josh says, "Granny, this is Ada."

"At last!" the lady says, stepping forwards and taking my hands. "I've heard so much about you and now, seeing you in person, I feel like I've met you before. I'm Biba," she says, adding unnecessarily, "Josh's grandmother."

Biba, I think. I don't think I've ever met a Biba before.

"It's really nice to meet you," I say. "I've heard a lot about you, too. And I believe you were born in Cornwall?"

"Yes, I was. Not all that far from here, in fact," she says. "Now, I believe you've very kindly offered to drive us to the hotel?"

"Nice and direct, Granny," Josh says.

"Well, no point beating around the bush, is there? I'm exhausted after that journey."

"It's not like you were driving the train. You just sat there and drank tea and talked, and talked, and talked…"

"Josh!" I say, mock-outraged, pleased to see Biba laughing. It seems like my friend has been lucky with his grandmother as I have with mine. "Come on, let's get to the car. Can I take your bag, Biba?"

"No need, it's got wheels." She pulls the handle of her case and begins to walk. I can see it's going to take a while despite the wheels but there's no rush. Even so, I feel a bit of a spare part, and like people might judge me, walking along with my free arms swinging by my side while my elderly companion drags her heavy case along behind herself.

Biba sits in the passenger seat and Josh is in the back. I can't wait to have the chance to really chat with him but for now this is very much about his grandmother. It must be strange coming back to somewhere you haven't been for decades.

"Well, well, well," she says every now and then or, "Would you look at that."

"Does it seem very different?" I ask.

"No, not really. Well, I don't think so. I suppose that we didn't come down into the town very often. It was quite a sheltered childhood in many ways. I need to get my bearings. But I am so tired now. I wonder if you'd mind if I have a rest once we're at the hotel? I'm sure you two can find something to occupy yourselves without me slowing you down."

"You feel free to do whatever you like," I say. "You wouldn't be slowing us down."

"I think we both know that's not true!" she laughs. "But it's kind of you to say so. I can see why you and Josh get on so well. Both kind souls. Despite the cheek, Joshua."

I glance in the mirror to see Josh smiling. I smile back. I know I've already said this, but it is so good to see him.

I hadn't expected much of a reaction from Biba at the sight of Tregynon Manor. After all, these kind of places are part and parcel of her world. I imagine most of the people she knows live in great big houses like this. Even so, she takes a deep breath as we enter the driveway. I suppose it is a bit special, set up high above the sea.

"It's nice, isn't it?" I ask, internally kicking myself for the 'nice', which gran says is one of the most ineffective and shallow ways to describe something.

"It's beautiful," Biba says.

"Incredible," says Josh.

"I think so." I pull up to the front door so that Biba doesn't have too far to walk, and I'm glad to see that she lets Josh carry her case up the steps. I find a parking space and go into the lobby to find them checking in.

"We'll just go up and find our rooms," says Josh. "Do you want to go through to the bar and I'll come and meet you in a bit?"

"Sounds like a good idea."

"Ada," Biba says, "would you care to join us here for dinner tonight?"

"I'd love that!" I smile.

"Super."

"Have a good rest," I say.

"Thank you, dear."

I order a lemonade and take it out to one of the tables on the patio, messaging Josh so he knows where to find me. It's funny to think that so many years ago my own grandmother would have been here. I imagine how strange it must have been, arriving for the first time. She had never seen the sea before coming to Cornwall.

"Ada!" I hear behind me and I stand and hug Josh again.

Without Biba behind him, I hold onto him for a little bit longer. "I've missed you."

"I've missed you too. It's so good to be here. And look at this place, and this weather! Beautiful." He tries out a Cornish accent. It is terrible.

"Don't do that around the town," I say, "you'll get mobbed."

"I'll bear that in mind. Look, let me get a beer and I'll be right back."

As it happens, a waiter is passing and says he'll get Josh's drink so the two of us sit down.

"So…" Josh says.

"So…"

"How are you doing? After all that with Archie?"

"Oh, it's all in the past now," I say breezily.

"Ada…"

"It is," I insist. "It has to be. I'm an idiot. You were so right, I should have known. I probably did know, really, all along. I just let myself get a bit carried away."

"I'll say," he raises his eyebrows.

"I don't mean like that! But yeah, like that as well."

"Has he been in touch?"

"A couple of times."

"I think he feels like a real shit, you know. In fact, this is as much remorse as I've seen from Archie Kingston."

"Really?"

"Really. But that doesn't mean you can go back to fancying him."

"I don't suppose I've stopped fancying him," I say, "I just know that it's a ridiculous idea and I should never have acted on it."

"Don't sweat it. These things happen. Move on."

"Anyway, how about you? Are you alright?"

"Yes, I've just been dying of boredom at home."

"Have you not been keeping up with your embroidery and piano practice?"

"Ada, I do not live in *Pride and Prejudice*! And I don't appreciate the insinuation that I am girly. If I was a Jane Austen character I'd be gallivanting around the countryside on a stallion, breaking the hearts of all the local maidens."

"Sure."

"Honestly, though, it's deathly dull. I need to do something. Andrew's busy with managing the estate and learning the ropes, as he puts it. Ma and Pa are on about moving to Spain in the not-too-distant future and want to leave the place in Andrew's hands. I could help him but what's the point, really? It doesn't really interest me. You know it's not the life for me and besides, it's Andrew who's set to inherit it all. I need to find my own thing. And that, as it turns out, is what Granny wanted to talk to me about."

"Really?"

"Yes. It's, well I'm a bit embarrassed really because I know it's ridiculous, but she wants to help me buy somewhere to live – or to start a business. She says it's not fair that Andrew should get everything. Her oldest brother managed to lose much of their family fortune, and she was lucky to have made a match that was to her advantage."

"And you say it's not all *Pride and Prejudice*."

"Alright, I'll let you have that one. But you know, it's the world I come from. I can't do anything about that."

"I know. Bloody hell, though!"

"I realise I'm being offered an amazing start in life, which I know is incredibly unfair and not something many people would ever have, but wouldn't I be mad to turn it down?"

"Well yes, you would," I say, feeling slightly envious and also worried this means I'll be left behind. I'd kind of hoped Josh and I would do something together.

"So I need to give it some thought. I've got a few ideas, and I'm hoping you can help me work it out while I'm here. Anyway, how's your work going?"

"Lifeguarding?"

"That, and your *real* work. Your art. You said you'd started something."

"Yes," I say, smiling, thinking of the mess of Gran's attic. "I feel like this idea's been brewing for a while and now I've set it in motion. I'm really excited about it."

"Can I see what you've done?"

"Yes, of course. As long as you don't tell anyone about it. And Gran will be so pleased to see you. We'd better go and see Mum, too. Shall we do all that tomorrow? Right now I feel like sitting out here in this beautiful garden with you and pretending we live here."

"Together?"

"Well, you as my butler of course."

"Of course. So anyway, how is lifeguarding too? Any gorgeous boys?"

"Not too bad," I say, "on both counts. And I'm getting to know a few of the others now, which is nice because my only other friend here is fourteen."

"Stevie?"

"Yes," I smile. "She's dying to meet you too."

"It's like a celebrity visiting town, I imagine."

"Just like that."

"I'm glad you're making friends, though."

"Yeah, it's good." I don't tell him I've had to turn down a night out tonight to be with him. Nic, one of the girls I work with, who has also recently graduated, asked me along. "I'd love to go next time," I told her, hoping that there will be a next time. I do need to try and fit in for as long as I am here. Which, unless I have any major brainwaves, could be some time. I don't know what will happen in October, when I'm unlikely to be needed for work, but we'll cross that bridge when we come to it.

Josh orders a bottle of prosecco and I say I'll have a glass but then Mum phones and says that she and Jude can walk up and collect the car, so I have a second glass.

"You just couldn't wait to see Josh!" I say, smiling as Mum and Jude appear.

"I'm not ashamed to admit it," says Mum, hugging Josh who has stood to greet her. "Here he is, the son I never had!"

"Bloody hell, Mum," I say but it makes me laugh.

They stay on for a drink and then get on their way. By this time I'm feeling a bit tipsy so I switch to water, not wanting to be drunk when Biba comes to join us. I'm glad I made this decision because when she does arrive, she's ordered us all martinis.

"They tell me this is their house speciality. Although I see you two have been partaking already," she says, eyeing up the empty glasses.

"We've just had a couple, Granny," says Josh.

I am grateful for the bread and olives and salted almonds that are brought to us, and the fact that Biba wants to eat quite early.

"I'm still feeling quite tired," she says.

"Are you sure you're alright?" Josh asks, concerned. It makes me think of Gran and I hope she's alright. She wasn't expecting to see us today but I do pop in most days.

"I'm fine darling, thank you. It's just, well, it's a bit overwhelming being here." She pauses and takes a sip of her drink. "I didn't tell you, Joshua, but this–" she gestures to the grand building behind us – "is actually where I lived when I was a child."

"No!" he says, theatrically.

"Yes."

"But why didn't you say?"

"I suppose it's a bit silly but we left under a bit of a shadow. You know, of course, about my brother managing to lose the whole estate through his recklessness. But even before that, we had a bit of a reputation around here. Daddy did, anyway."

"Oh no," says Josh. "Really?"

"Yes, and I just wasn't sure, if I wanted to come back, or how I'd feel when I did. But I'm here, and I'm just another paying guest. Only it's raked up a lot of feelings."

I just listen to this exchange, my brain whirring, but unwilling to interrupt such a personal conversation. I have, after all, only met Biba for the first time today. I marvel that she is being so open in front of me. Only when Josh has excused himself to go to the loo do I ask the question that's been forming.

"Biba," I say, and she looks at me. "Is your name short for Tabitha?"

2021

Eventually, summer came around again and finally, truly, life was getting back to how it had been before Covid. People were allowed to travel abroad again and some wasted no time, although there were regularly changes to the list of countries people were allowed to visit so Cornwall was once again heaving with holiday-makers who didn't want to risk disappointment.

"How much?" Clara exclaimed, as Elise told her and Ada about a recent offer made on her house.

"I know!" laughed Elise. "I thought they were pulling my leg. They're still not having it, though."

"Good for you, Gran," said Ada.

"Well, Angela entrusted me with this place and I want to be able to pass it on too, one day."

Ada supposed the house would go to her mum and Uncle Laurie eventually, though her mum was certainly not in need of it. Would Laurie ever return to Cornwall? It seemed unlikely – so would that mean he'd just sell the house anyway? Whatever, it was none of her business, and certainly nothing to bother Elise about.

It was so good to be back there after missing the previous year and the girls had wasted no time in going to the beach. Ada had expected Elise to look older, and more frail, but in actual fact she seemed happy, and she looked well. She had a new friend called Maggie, who was younger even than Louisa, and it seemed that Maggie and her young daughter Stevie had been spending a lot of time with Elise.

A brief thought had passed fleetingly through Ada's

mind: what if they were after her gran's house? Opportunists taking advantage of an elderly lady? But then she met the pair of them and that certainly didn't seem to be the case. She gave herself a mental telling off for even thinking that way. It was Elise's mention of passing the house on that had got the thought of inheritance in her head and she hated herself for it. Nothing like that mattered; it was her gran's health and happiness that were important.

"Remember when we used to say we'd live here when we were grown-ups?" Ada asked Clara, as they lay side by side on the beach, bodies still glistening with saltwater.

Clara laughed. "Oh yeah! We had no idea, did we? I mean, I love coming for a holiday, but there's not exactly a lot to do, is there? Once you take away the beach, I mean. And you can't spend every day on the beach. How would you earn a living round here?"

"Gran's paid for me to train as a lifeguard," Ada reminded her, "so actually I could work and be on the beach every day."

"It's not exactly a long-term thing though, is it?" Clara laughed. "No, I think I'd go mad if I wasn't in a city. Joe and I were talking and we're thinking we might stay in Birmingham when we graduate. I might do a Master's…"

"Really?" This was news to Ada, and sent a slight panic through her that she had not thought that far ahead, and that her friend seemed to be making plans with her boyfriend so far into the future.

"Yeah. Well, maybe. You know. It's a long way off yet. But I like the idea…"

"With Joe?"

"Yes. Definitely."

"I'm glad you've met somebody you like so much."

"I do." Clara turned her head and looked at Ada, her eyes shining. "You'll like him too, when you meet."

"I'm sure I will." Ada, lying on her front, put her head on her arms, feeling the warmth of her skin and breathing in its soft, salty smell. She listened to the sounds of the busy beach, and the relaxed laughter and chatter of families and groups of friends set free after so long constrained and contained at home.

She thought of Ben, and how she had never told Clara about him. How her friend probably thought she was naïve and inexperienced. If only she knew. But, though she did trust Clara, it felt like it was really somebody else's secret she'd be giving away. It was Ben who would have his life thrown into turmoil if the truth ever got out.

He'd be married by now, she supposed, and she idly wondered if he and Amber would go on to have a family. All of that seemed a long way off to her; she felt far too young, though she knew Elise must have been not much older than her when she got married and started a family. Louisa had been much older, of course, when she had her. And she'd skipped the getting married bit; the whole relationship part, in fact.

It was a strange thought that Ada's dad was out there somewhere and he didn't know about her. But there was nothing she could do, unless she wanted to try and track him down, and she didn't think she wanted to do that.

She glanced across at Clara, who was lying on her back, sunglasses on and a smile on her face. Thinking about Joe, no doubt. Ada lay her head back down and allowed her eyes to shut once more. With the sound of the sea and the gulls and the happy shouts of children providing a soundtrack, she drifted off into a light, sunny sleep.

"Excuse me ladies," came a voice and Clara sat up, suddenly on her guard.

"Yes?" She looked up and saw a tall, good-looking older man. He seemed out of place on the beach, dressed in smart trousers and a shirt, though he'd unbuttoned the collar and rolled up his sleeves.

"I'm sorry to bother you. But aren't you Louisa's daughter?" He addressed Ada.

Ada sat up too, drawing her knees up in front of her.

"I'm... yes."

"Who's asking?"

Clara and Ada spoke at the same time, Clara sensibly more defensive and suspicious.

Ada felt underdressed in her bikini, and she folded her arms in front of her chest.

The man just smiled. "I thought I recognised you from her pictures. I'm AJ, I work with Louisa," he said, and he held out his hand. Ada took it. "Maybe she hasn't mentioned me?"

"Erm, no, I think she has."

"Oh, good. Well, I'm down here working and I saw you and I just thought I'd come and say hello. It's a pleasure to meet you."

And with that, he was gone. The girls watched him walk towards a woman in a smart dress, her feet bare but a pair of high-heeled shoes in her hand. She said something to AJ and glanced towards the girls. Ada saw him take the woman's hand and kiss it, laughing as she drew it away in an irritated fashion.

"Well, that was weird," said Clara.

"Really weird!" Ada agreed, and the two of them returned to their sunbathing.

Ada

I don't want to cut short my evening but I am bursting to get back to Gran and tell her what I've discovered, or think I've discovered. I need to check I'm right about this, and also – assuming I am – whether I should tell Biba who my gran is. Her alluding to her dad's reputation suggests she knows about his wandering eye (and hands). Maybe she will blame Gran for her part in her family's fall from grace.

So I have to bite my tongue, and make pleasant conversation, although it isn't that hard; it is a really nice evening and Biba is full of questions about the local area and about me too.

She shows a real interest in my degree. "Art and anthropology – do they go together?"

"Well yes and no. I mean, my interest is always in people and I suppose my art reflects that. I studied art history but I took some fine art modules too and I loved being part of the art society. We both did, didn't we Josh?"

"I did, but I think it's more up your street than mine. You're the one with the talent, Ada. I just enjoy dipping my toe in the water. Or my brush in the paint."

"You are way too hard on yourself, Josh. Do you know," I say to Biba, "before I met Josh, I had no idea how to cook – or very little idea, anyway. My mum was always at work and we used to exist on ready meals. Really nice ones, you know, from M&S and Waitrose, that kind of thing…" I feel my words begin to falter as I wonder if she actually does know that kind of thing but she smiles and nods so I continue. "I realised through Josh that it's actually possible to make these things instead, and that they taste just as good, they cost half as much, and they're probably much more healthy too."

"I don't know where he gets it from!" Biba says. "Certainly not his parents. Or from me! But I know he's a whizz in the kitchen."

"You're making me blush," Josh says but I can see he's enjoying himself.

"Really," I say seriously, "if I hadn't met Josh, the last three years would have been nowhere near as good."

"He's a good boy," Biba says. "He'll make somebody a lovely husband."

Josh and I look at each other.

"Gran!" he exclaims. "What a thing to say."

"But it's true!" she protests.

"Maybe I don't want to make somebody a lovely husband."

"That would be such a waste though, darling!"

Josh groans.

"Alright!" she laughs. "I get the message." But she winks at me, and I blush.

I remember my conversation with Gran, about relationships, and I'm in awe of her all over again, at her ability to look beyond the immediate, the expected, and accepted, way of the world.

I can see what Biba is doing here; let's face it, she's not exactly trying to hide it. And she's not done yet.

"I will just say, to both of you, that if you have a chance at happiness with somebody, you should take it. My own parents were not in the least bit happy together. I've been lucky and your parents have too, Joshua. And I can see how much you two mean to each other. I just don't want you to miss the boat."

I don't know what to say. I am grateful that my own grandmother would not put me in this situation, but I know that Biba means well. I just smile at Josh and he rolls his eyes.

"I saw that, Joshua," Biba says. "And I'm sorry, I shouldn't interfere."

"Correct," says Josh.

"I'll consider that my wrist slapped," she says. "Now, Ada, I hope you're going to have dessert, and you can tell me about the best places to buy property around here."

"Oh," I say, looking at my watch. "I really ought to get back. And I'm much too full for dessert," I say, patting my tummy. I am keen to get to Gran's before she goes to bed. "As for buying property, I'd say anywhere is a good bet around here, but it gets more expensive around Carbis Bay and St Ives. Are you looking for yourself? Do you think you'd move back?"

"Maybe," she says and she smiles at Josh and I know exactly what she's thinking.

"I'm so sorry about Granny," Josh says as we walk back along the dark road together, keeping alert for traffic.

"That's OK!" I say. "She's just looking out for you."

"I know. But it's embarrassing."

"It's fine," I say, sliding my arm into the crook of his. "It's how people are. Most people," I correct myself.

"Just because you're a girl and I'm a boy, and we get on so well… I think she believes in fate, and people being brought together by the universe."

"It's how people make sense of the world," I say, and I'm keen to continue this conversation as it feels like Josh is going to open up a little for once. But I'm also thinking of Gran and of Biba, and how crazy that link is. I don't disagree that the universe does seem to bring people together sometimes, and I do think Josh and I were meant to meet, but could the real reason for that be a connection that goes back way into the last century? Time will tell.

As the pavement returns and streetlights come into view, I turn to Josh. "I'll be fine from here. You get going, it's all uphill from here you know."

"Are you sure?"

"Of course! It's you I'm worried about, going back through the dark again. Drop me a line to let me know you're back at the hotel safely, please."

We reach the first streetlight and hug, then I send him on his way and I hurry on down to Gran's. I am so excited about telling her my news. I imagine taking her up to Tregynon tomorrow; orchestrating an emotional reunion. But I also know she might just want to keep the past in the past. And besides, Biba might not even really remember her. I guess Gran was one of a long run of nannies, governesses and so on, many of whom went the same way.

Gran's curtains are closed but I can see the light is on in her front room so I knock gently on the door and push it open.

"It's just me, Gran," I say so as not to startle her, although to be fair she is made of pretty tough stuff.

The house is in silence though, and as I walk into the lounge there's no sign of her.

"Gran?" I call. No reply.

I walk around the house, which doesn't take long. I check the bathroom but it's empty, and her bedroom is in darkness, the door open. I switch on the light just to check, and she's not there.

My heart is thudding a little but I remind myself of her tendency towards night-time walks, and her habit of not locking her door, which Mum regularly tells her off about.

What should I do? Go and look for her, wait for her to return, or go back to Mum's and pretend that I wasn't here? After all, the first two options mean that Gran will know I know about her night-time walks. And I feel as though she likes them being a secret. But I can't quite let myself leave here without knowing she is back home safe and sound. I sit down and wait.

The ticking of the clock counts out the seconds, and minutes, and there is still no sign of Gran. I can't wait any longer. I am still brimming with excitement at the thought of telling her about Biba. I'm going to have to go and find her. I can always make out it's a coincidence. Feign surprise when I see her.

Crossing the road, I marvel at Gran's fearlessness, taking herself off and out in the darkness. I am not so brave and if I didn't know that she was out here, I wouldn't be venturing this way. I pick my way carefully down the steps, holding onto the handrail, wondering how on earth Gran has managed this. Perhaps she took the longer route, going down the slope to the beach.

I take a moment to focus my eyes when I reach the sand. The sea sounds louder in the darkness but the moon lends a little bit of light which illuminates the white tops of the waves as they roll in towards the shore and break open. I cast my eyes along the length of the beach but there is no sign of Gran, or of anybody else.

I shiver.

This is a familiar place to me, and even more so now that I've been working here. I know the location of all the rocks and as we are almost at high tide right now, most of them are obscured by the water. There are just a few smaller ones, conveniently situated for people to sit and pull on beach shoes or swimming socks, or to drape towels and dry robes ready for returning from the sea. But there is a smaller, unexpected, dark shape on the sand, down near the shore, and I am sure it's not a rock. I begin to walk quickly towards it, terrified because even from this distance I think I know what I am going to find. I break into a jog and I can see it is what I feared. A person, lying on the sand.

"Hello?" I shout, thinking maybe it's just somebody having a rest; worse, a pair of people lying together. As I get closer, the shape becomes more defined and I start to sprint towards it. Towards her. Because I can see without a doubt that it's my gran. She is lying on the beach, and she's not moving.

2021

Ada had been sitting in her room studying when her phone began to ring. She almost didn't answer but something made her pick up.

"Ada?" Her mum's voice sounded artificially cheerful.

"Mum? Is everything alright?" Ada asked, heart beating fast, wondering if Louisa might be ill. She had become increasingly aware of Louisa's age over recent years, particularly in contrast with most of her friends' parents, like Andy and Mary who were only just into their fifties.

"Well, yes and no," Louisa had tried to laugh. "Listen, Ada, I don't know how to tell you this…"

It was cancer, wasn't it? It was bound to be. Ada's heart was pounding so hard she nearly didn't hear what her mum had said. She had to ask her to repeat herself.

"I'm selling up," Louisa said awkwardly. "Leaving London. For Cornwall."

Ada was speechless.

"I'm sorry Ada, I know it's a shock. It wasn't… well it wasn't what I'd planned, but I've had to leave work and…"

"Leave work?" Ada was finding it hard to keep up.

"Yes."

"You've had to? What do you mean?"

"Well, there's been a… change of personnel."

"You've been fired?"

"I've – not exactly."

Louisa had gone on to explain that the project in Cornwall was being progressed without her and there was no longer any role for her in the business. It all sounded a bit ridiculous to Ada, but what did she know?

"The upshot of it is though, Ada, I've decided I need to make some major changes, and I need to be near Mum as well. She's getting on, you know, and I haven't always been there. And I know it will be strange for you, but you've left home now—"

"I've only gone to uni! I was planning on coming back for visits, and I don't know what I'll be doing after I graduate…" Ada's words tailed off, limply.

"I know. I know all that, darling. And wherever I am, there will always be a place for you. But I can't stay in London. I just can't."

My god, was her mum crying? Ada couldn't stand the thought of that.

"It's alright, Mum. It's fine. I mean, it's a bit of a shock, but you can't just stay there for my visits home. And you're right, about Gran. She'll be so pleased to have you near. And you know I like Cornwall. Love it, in fact."

Was she overdoing it? The positivity? Ada was just trying to find the right things to say. It was going to take her a lot longer to get her head round all of this than she was making out, but she didn't want her mum to feel bad on her behalf.

"Oh Ada, what have I done to deserve you? Thank you for making this so easy."

"It's fine, Mum. As long as you're OK."

"I am now I've spoken to you."

After she'd hung up, Ada tried to get back to her work but she couldn't focus so she went in search of Sasha, and was pleased to find Archie and Josh were in the living room.

"Cuppa?" called Sasha from the kitchen.

"Yes please."

Archie smiled and patted the seat next to him. She accepted the offer, settling onto the vacant seat but curling her knees away from him. Aware that they had both been in the same lecture about body language, she was at pains not to give herself away.

She wanted to tell them about her mum's news but she thought she might burst into tears so she kept it to herself and let her friends' company wash over her, taking her mind off things. The afternoon passed by with her other flatmates returning home and all of them squeezing into the living room, opening cans of beer and passing round a joint that Archie rolled; playing cards and discussing important matters like the merits of biscuits.

"Bourbons," Archie proclaimed, "are very much under-rated."

"My gran hates them," said Ada.

"How can you hate Bourbons?" Sasha cried indignantly.

"Dunno. She likes mint Clubs."

"Urgh. Why would you put toothpaste on a biscuit?" Josh said.

"You'll have to ask my gran."

Will, a lad from one of the other nearby flats, knocked on the door and Charlotte let him in. "You can hear you lot all the way down the corridor!" he said.

"We'd better try and keep it down a bit," said Ada, aware they weren't really adhering to the rules about visitors. "This must have been what it was like in the old days, when you weren't allowed to have members of the opposite sex over."

"And certainly not overnight!" said Charlotte, kissing Will and pulling him towards her room.

"That's the last we'll see of them," said Josh. "How about some food? I'm starving. I can whip up a veggie chilli and some rice if you fancy it."

"That sounds great," said Ada. "I'll help."

She didn't really want to lose her seat next to Archie but she knew that she could tell Josh about the phone call with her mum. Out of all her new friends, he was the one she found it easiest to talk to.

She thought of Clara and their promise to each other. *Friends first.* She really ought to call her and tell her the news too. Her stomach sank as she thought of her friend, and Mary and Andy; Lily and Harry. Clara's family were an extension of Ada's but if Louisa was selling up in London, how would she be able to spend time with them again? The life she knew was changing rapidly, and there was nothing she could do about it.

Ada

Mum is grey-faced as she comes back into the hospital room. In fact, I've never seen her look so worried.

"Thank God you found her, Ada!" she says. "What on earth was she doing on the beach on her own? In the middle of the night!"

"Ssh," I say, looking at Gran. Hooked up to a drip and some kind of machine, she is fast asleep right now but I'm sure she might still be able to hear us. "She's alright now, isn't she?"

Mum looks at Jude, who has followed her in. My stomach sinks.

"I don't know about that, my love." Mum puts her arm around me. "Gran's really poorly, you know. She's safe and looked after now, thanks to you, but I don't know. I'm not sure she'll be coming home. We'll see."

It's unlike Mum to be selecting her words so carefully. She is generally very direct.

"Is that what the doctor said?" I ask.

I haven't been told anything much, as Gran was whisked away and I was left sitting in the waiting room, and then Mum and Jude arrived, and Mum took over.

"Yes, and she also said it was very fortunate that you found Mum when you did, or she'd have died there on the beach."

This is the Mum I know. She's always said not to use phrases like 'passed away' – to be clear and honest about death. And it's how I know now that Gran really isn't going to be coming home.

"They say they've made her comfortable," Jude says, squeezing Mum's hand.

"She looks comfortable." I try a small smile, and I stroke Gran's hair. She stirs a little.

"She does, doesn't she?" says Mum. "But she looks so small as well," she half-wails.

"She's always been small!" I smile. "You're not exactly Miranda Hart yourself." This at least gets a little laugh. In fact, if I'm not mistaken, I see Gran's mouth twitch too.

"Mum," I say. "I think she can hear us."

Gran's eyelids flutter a little. They look so thin and delicate. And then she is looking at us through her beautiful blue eyes which seem a little faded and cloudy.

"I can," she croaks. "I can hear you."

"Oh Mum," my own mum says, and she leans across the bed to hug my gran. "Mum."

"Ssh," Gran says. "Hush now, my girl. I'm quite alright."

Do we tell her, I wonder. Or has she already heard what Mum said, about her coming so close to dying on the beach? I think we all know she is not alright but who's going to say that?

I feel really young all of a sudden, and inexperienced. I've never been around somebody so ill before, and certainly not somebody who is dying.

"Sorry to be causing this fuss," says Gran. "I'd hoped to slip away quietly when the time came."

I look down at my hands, pressing them together hard and squeezing my eyes shut, trying to hold back the tears. I feel Jude move closer to me, putting her hand on mine. I know she's no stranger to grief, her son having died at a very young age. I wonder what this is like for her and I look at her and try to smile. Her face is just full of clear concern for me and I feel a rush of love for her. I'm so glad that she and Mum found each other.

In fact, it sounds a little bit clichéd, but the room feels full of love right now. It's almost tangible. I picture my great-gran, Annabel, and Gran's dad, standing by her. Angels and soft light. I barely dare look at her. Is she about to die, right now?

She pulls herself up a little. Apparently not.

"Here, Mum," my mum offers Gran her arm to use as a lever, and she arranges the pillows behind Gran's head so that she is slightly elevated.

"Thank you, my girl," says Gran, gazing at my mum with such tenderness.

"Laurie's coming," Mum says. "He's on his way."

"Really?" Gran's eyes light up a little.

"Really."

"I'd better hang on then," Gran says. "Can't go popping off before he gets here." She lets out a raspy cough, which seems to not want to let her go. Mum helps her sit forward a little until the coughing has stopped, and then Gran sinks back, exhausted.

"How is Josh?" Gran asks me. "I'm sorry to have ruined his visit."

"Gran!" I laugh, despite tears pricking at my eyes. I can't believe she is apologising, thinking of others even in this moment. "He's good thanks. And his gran…"

I think of Biba and how I'd been so eager to get back to Gran and tell her what I'd found out, but I hadn't wanted to be rude and leave the hotel too early. What if I had, though? Would things be any different? Gran would have stayed in and we'd have stayed up chatting, till it was so late she'd have just gone to bed. I could kick myself for not getting to her more quickly.

"Tell him I'm sorry I won't see him," Gran says, and she reaches her hand towards me. I lean forward and take it. "And don't forget our chat from the other night, will you?"

"I won't. I promise."

Her eyelids flicker a little and she sighs, but it seems to me a contented sigh. I look at Mum, in a panic. She returns my look. Leans forward and peers at Gran's face.

Gran's eyes open again. "I thought it had gone dark," she says with a little laugh. "I'm not gone yet. Not going anywhere..."

But she does soon fall asleep again. Mum gestures to the door and I follow her out, Jude right behind me.

"They said she's hypothermic, and she's got a urine infection too, which is probably the reason she went out this evening. They can make you feel a bit confused when you're older."

"Can't they give her antibiotics?" I ask.

"Yes, and they're treating her hypothermia as well, but we have to prepare ourselves, Ada. She's very old now and quite weak. I'm sure you've noticed, she's not the same as she was even last year."

"I know," I say sadly.

"But she's alright, Ada. She's safe and being cared for, and we're here."

"Is there no chance she's going to recover?"

"I don't think so, no. I'm not a doctor, and I suppose things can happen that surprise us. But I don't know how long she was out on that beach, and her body temperature's low, plus she's trying to fight this infection. There might be other underlying things going on too. I know it sounds like I'm being very pessimistic and I don't mean to be. But Mum is a realist and I try to be too. There's no point pretending everything's OK when it isn't."

She hugs me and I lean into her.

"I love her," I sniff.

"I know you do. I do too. We're very lucky to have her."

"Will Uncle Laurie get here in time?"

"He set off early this morning so hopefully he won't be too long now. And if Mum has anything to do with it, yes he will get here in time," Mum smiles. "And you know how determined she is when it comes to people she loves."

"She is," I smile. And then I think of Josh, and of Biba, and I have an idea.

After a long morning, Mum and Jude and I eat lunch in the little hospital café, in shifts, one of us sitting in with Gran at all times so that she's never on her own. She sleeps for the most part but does have moments of wakefulness, though at times it seems she is just staring off into nothingness.

I am on edge and not entirely comfortable when I'm on my own with her. What if something happens? What if she dies when it's just her and me?

And then she seems to rally around a little again and the timing couldn't be better, because just as Mum is setting a cardigan around Gran's shoulders, there is a knock at the door. One of the nurses pops her head in. "You've got visitors, Elise," she says.

"Josh!" I say as my friend steps into the room, followed by his grandmother.

"Biba," I step forward and take her hands. "Thank you."

She is smiling but looking past me, to my gran. I turn to look as well and see that despite everything; her frail, birdlike frame and the thinness of her hair, while she looks like she is being swallowed up by the hospital bed, my gran's smile stands out and tells me it's her, and she is still with us.

"Hello Josh my love," she says, accepting a gentle kiss from him.

"Hello Elise," he says. "I've brought somebody to see you. This is my grandmother ..."

Biba steps forward. "Hello Elise."

The two women look at each other.

"I..." Gran says, as if trying to work something out.

"It's Tabitha," I say, unable to help myself. "This is Tabitha."

"Tabitha?" Gran says. "Not..."

"Yes," Biba says gently.

Gran's resolve and bravery crumble. Her face seems to collapse, and she is soon awash with tears.

Mum moves out of her seat and gestures to Biba, who moves forward and sits, taking Gran's hand in both of hers.

"It's alright," she says kindly. "It's quite alright."

"But you can't..." Gran looks from Biba to Mum, to me.

"She's Josh's grandmother," I explain. "I only realised yesterday. And I was coming to tell you, only..."

209

"It's too much for her," Mum says. "We shouldn't have…"

"You certainly should!" Gran says now, a flash of strength zapping into her. "You should. You really should." She gazes at Biba's face. "I can see it now. I can see you."

I realise Biba is also in tears. "I never forgot you, Elise. You taught me to swim!" she laughs. "You were so kind. And I thought… I thought you were so beautiful. I wanted to be like you when I grew up."

"But I left you," says Gran.

"You had to," Biba says. "They told me you had to look after your aunt and had to leave suddenly. I was distraught. So were the boys…"

"The boys," Gran says. "How are they… are they?"

"Edmond is in Scotland," Biba says. "I'm afraid Charles died some years ago."

"Oh," says Gran, looking stricken.

"Edmond sends his love though. Honestly, I had no idea; not until your beautiful, clever granddaughter telephoned my Joshua just this morning. I had to sit down, didn't I Josh? Otherwise I'm sure I'd have fallen over."

"It's true!" Josh grins. "We were out looking at… just having a little explore really and the next thing I knew, Ada was calling, and asking to speak to Granny, who went very pale."

Gran is looking pale herself, and very tired. Her eyes are shadowed by purple half-moons.

"Maybe we should go," Biba says.

"No, stay," Gran murmurs. "A little longer. Tell me what you've done with your life."

Biba looks around at Mum, aware that she might be trespassing on precious moments but Mum just smiles and nods. She moves to the chair at the other side of Gran's bed.

"Josh," I say, "would you come with me? I need a hand with something."

"Of course," he says.

Once we are out of Gran's room, he takes my hand and once we are safely out of earshot I fall against him, my body heaving with great, wracking sobs.

When we return to Gran's room, she is sleeping once more and Biba is standing near the door.

"We really should go now darling," she says to Josh.

"Of course." He looks at me and squeezes my hand. "I'll call you later."

"Thank you," I say. "And thank you, Biba, for this."

"It was my pleasure. I never have forgotten your grandmother, you know. We had a lot of people come and go through our childhood, some nicer than others. She was one of the best. I'm so glad to have had the chance to see her again. I'm just so sorry for you all, now…"

"I know," I say. I look at Mum, and she offers a small, hopeless smile.

Kissing Biba on the cheek, I watch her and Josh walk along the corridor until they are out of sight, and then I sit down in the chair Biba has vacated.

"I'm going to get us some drinks," Jude says. "I'll be back soon." She opens the door and says, "Oh, sorry – oh… Laurie!"

And he is here, my uncle – tall and ungainly and very much greying these days. He stoops as he comes into the room, though the door is not that low. I suppose that perhaps this has become a necessary habit in the little house he lives in on his Scottish island.

"Laurie!" Mum cries and she stands and flings herself at him. He holds her and kisses her hair, but he's looking towards the small, frail figure in the bed.

"Oh," he sobs. "Oh, Mum."

I kiss Gran and stand up. "Have this seat, Uncle Laurie."

"Oh Ada," he looks as though he's only just noticed me. "Thank you. Are you alright? You found her, you hero!"

"I don't know about that. And yes, I'm OK thank you. She was so pleased to hear that you were on your way."

"I thought I'd be too late." He looks to Mum, as though she's the older sibling.

"She's still with us," she reassures him. "Go and see her."

I move out of the way and Laurie sits down, looking at his mum and then putting the back of his hand against her cheek.

"I'll come with you," I say to Jude. "Shall I get you a coffee, Laurie?"

"Yes please my sweet, that would be much appreciated."

So Jude and I make ourselves scarce, leaving Gran with her two children for a while. Back to how it was after my grandad died and it was just the three of them.

"Would you like some fresh air?" Jude asks me. "Before we get the drinks?"

"That sounds like a good idea," I say.

We go through the automatic doors, emerging into a

day which feels far too full of life and warmth after the cool, clinical interior of the hospital.

"How are you doing?" Jude asks me.

"Oh, I don't know." I hadn't really thought about it but I realise I feel drained, and my eyes ache. My head, too.

"Let's just sit for a while." She gestures to a grassy slope, which is patchy and dried out from the summer sun. "Shall we?"

"Yes please."

"You did very well to find her, you know."

"Well, it was just luck really."

"I don't know, it feels like that whole thing – Josh and his grandma, and you piecing that bit of history together – was all meant to happen like it did. Otherwise you might have just gone back to the flat and Elise might not have been found until this morning. She could easily have died out there. You've given your mum, and your uncle, and yourself the chance to say your goodbyes. And you gave your gran some closure as well, bringing Tabitha back to her. Honestly, you couldn't have done things better."

I lean back against the grass, briefly allowing myself a moment of inward congratulation.

Jude lies back too. "Life's hard sometimes," she says. "Very hard."

"Yep."

"But it's beautiful too."

I gaze up at the clouds. Around us, there is traffic moving in and out of the hospital car park. Ambulances bringing in emergencies. Expectant mothers hobbling towards the maternity unit. There are people walking to appointments, some anticipating terrible news, some hoping for the best. Friends, wives, husbands, children, accompanying those they love, facing their own worst fears.

And inside that building is my gran. The strongest woman I know. A woman who has been through so much in her long life, and who I carry a part of now.

"Let's go back in," I say suddenly, standing. "I think we need to."

"Of course." Jude stands too, brushing a few stray blades of dried grass from her trousers.

I hurry on ahead and I reach Gran's room, and I push open the door to see Mum with her head on Gran's chest and Laurie looking across at us, like a lost little boy.

I stop in my tracks and I take it all in, the images and thoughts swimming through my head. There she is, my beautiful gran, except she's not.

My mum looks up with red-rimmed eyes and says what she doesn't need to tell me. "She's gone."

2021

By the time Christmas came around, Ada was really ready for a break. She was exhausted.

But she couldn't go home, she reminded herself. There was a new family living there these days, about to enjoy their first Christmas in their beautiful new house. It was their home now. It hadn't taken long at all for Louisa to sell the house. She had been ruthless in her 'downsizing' though she had kept everything of Ada's, and she had succumbed to a storage unit for some items she couldn't yet be parted from. Within a matter of weeks, however, after that phone call to Ada, Louisa had emptied the house – their house – and paid for the apartment in Cornwall, in cash. Ada had managed a quick, painful visit home to say goodbye and it all still felt very unreal.

And yet, despite everything, during the train journey to Cornwall, Ada began to feel a bit happier. There were small children sitting opposite her, their mum in the seat in front, and they couldn't stop talking about Christmas, and staying with Granny and Grandpa, and wondering how Father Christmas would know where they were. Their excitement was catching and Ada realised that she couldn't wait to be back with her mum and finally get to see this new apartment.

Louisa met her at the station. "I have missed you so much, Ada," she said, hugging her daughter tightly. "I didn't know it was possible to miss anybody this much."

"I don't blame you," Ada smiled. "I am pretty great."

"You are. And modest, too. Now come on, I'm parked on double yellows, and I don't want a ticket."

Ada thought her mum seemed more relaxed than she had done back home. She certainly looked less tired. Louisa had shared no more details about what had happened at work but it was clear that it had upset her. Was it something to do with her mum's age? That seemed about right to Ada; it was something they discussed a lot at uni.

As Louisa drove Ada through the dark afternoon, they both found themselves feeling a bit nervous; Louisa hoping her daughter would like the new place, and Ada scared that she might not. Still, gazing out of the window, Ada loved the sight of the small seaside town decked out in its Christmas sparkle.

The sea breeze hit her full-on as they rounded the corner to Louisa's building. On the harbourside the air held the faint tang of fish, and exhaust fumes from boat engines. And once they reached Louisa's apartment, she could see exactly why her mum had chosen it. It was upmarket without being overly flash, and it was so very different to their house in London. It was clear that Louisa was fully committed to starting her life afresh.

Ada gazed out of the window, looking down at the lights on the boats in the harbour, and way out across the deep, dark sea, to the lighthouse's intermittent signal.

They spent the first evening enjoying a meal and a film together as they had done so many times back home (as Ada could not help but think of it), only now it was cold and dark outside but there was no fire to light. Her mum's tree was new, too; a fake, ready-lit number which was classy and modern, but different to the real ones they'd had in London, which would fill the room with the scent of pine, and cover the floor with needles which they would still be finding for months into the following year.

They sat in their pyjamas, each glad to have the other's company once more, and keen to start to find a new balance in their world.

When Ada began to yawn, Louisa suggested they save the rest of the film for the following night. "Go on," she said, "nothing like your own bed."

But not my own room, Ada thought but didn't say. What would be the point? She hugged her mum then went into the strange room and looked around her, seeing familiar things but feeling a sudden urge to cry and thinking that she had never known the value of home until she didn't have it anymore.

Chastising herself for such self-pity, Ada got under the covers. And, despite everything, she realised that Louisa was right – there was nothing like your own bed. And she still had the same bedding, with the same familiar smell of the washing powder Louisa used. It was all just in a very different, strange place.

The apartment was so new, it was insulated to the nth degree, where their old house had been old and drafty. It started to feel a bit stifling and Ada felt the need to open the window for some fresh air. When she did, from somewhere amidst those little terraced streets just behind the harbour came the faint notes of people singing Christmas carols. And there it was as well, the sound of the sea.

There was no traffic noise here. No sirens. No trains rattling through. They formed the soundtrack she had grown up with back home and which had come to feel normal to her; a kind of comfort. Ada had liked the way they reminded her there was life going on all around her, especially on those nights when she found it hard to sleep.

But as the breeze entered her room now, stroking her face in greeting as it passed her by, Ada began to feel a little better. And she thought of the town just down below, and how her gran was only a couple of streets away, and that she'd be seeing her tomorrow.

It wasn't like she was a complete stranger in this place, Ada told herself. She had history here. She smiled to think of the holidays she'd had with Clara.

In the room next door, Louisa was shuffling about, getting ready for bed, and Ada felt a sudden rush of love for her mum. For years, she had thought Louisa didn't pay enough attention to Elise and now here she was, come home to roost. That thought made Ada happy. And really, who was she to complain about anything? She had left home, and she could not very well expect Louisa to just sit still, waiting for the times her daughter chose to grace her with a visit.

Ada closed her eyes, breathing in the beautiful air, then she turned and went back to her bed, pulling the covers up to her chin and falling into the deepest sleep she had known for quite some time.

Ada

The morning of Gran's funeral is misty and damp. I have had a restless night, as I have every night since she died. Mum has been the same; I know because we have more than once bumped into each other in the kitchen.

"Can't sleep?" she will ask, pulling her dressing gown around her and putting the kettle on.

"No," I will say, and put my arm around her. I've never been more aware of my mum's age than now. She is usually very smart and well put together, expert in making her face up so that it is hard to put a number on her. Since Gran died, Mum has barely bothered with make-up, and some days she has not even bothered to get dressed. It all depends on whether there is anything to get dressed for; appointments with funeral directors and the like offer her some motivation so that she seems a bit more like herself. Today, I know, she will pull herself together. We all will, for Gran.

"Could have done with you putting in a bit of effort though," I grumble at the sun, which I can dimly make out behind the cloud cover. It doesn't react, staying stubbornly concealed.

"Come on Ada," I chivvy myself along now, turning away from the window. "It's time to get moving."

I've hung my clothes on the handle of the wardrobe

door. A burnt amber dress and a dark green cardigan, should I need it. The colours seem fittingly autumnal. Although the summer has done itself proud this year, these last few days have been muted and subdued, calling for hoodies and jeans and even for closing the balcony doors in the evenings.

I shower and then dress, applying a little make-up and then assessing myself critically in the mirror.

I check the time. "You'll have to do," I say, and I take a deep breath and head out to the living area, where Mum and Jude and Uncle Laurie await.

Laurie has been staying at Gran's house and I wonder if it's strange without her there, but he seems to like it. Also he's been up to the flat most evenings for his tea, not minding at all if Mum's still in her pyjamas, or if it's spaghetti on toast again. None of us really have much appetite these days. Food has become functional, providing the energy we need but also a reason to come together when we might otherwise all be lost in our own little worlds.

"Is Jude coming with us?" I ask Mum.

"No, she's going to go with Maggie and Stevie."

"Oh, right. OK." Poor Maggie had been away when Gran died so she hadn't had a chance to say her goodbyes in person. Mum had tried to arrange a video call but it just wasn't going to happen, given how poorly Gran was. I think there used to be a little bit of friction between Maggie and Mum but as they've got to know each other, they've become close. And it's funny, how similar they are in looks. Lots of people comment on it, though Mum and Maggie both say they don't see it.

"And Josh will be there? And Biba?"

"Yes," I say. We both know all the arrangements of course, but we're finding a way to fill the silence that would otherwise pervade the space.

Laurie, meanwhile, stays quiet, just watching out of the window. I follow his line of sight and see a formation of five gulls, which cross the sky, taking their time and each taking a turn at wheeling in and back on themselves in graceful, looping movements.

"They're just magical," he says to me. "I know people hate them. They are much maligned, like pigeons."

"People often don't see the real beauty in things," Mum says, putting her hand on his arm. I feel like she is talking about him. I know Mum thinks her brother is underappreciated and I also know that she saw him go through some hard times growing up. It's funny, how very different they are but how close they are too, and how deeply they love each other.

"Come on," I say. "The car will be coming soon."

We leave the flat and I'm the last one out, pulling the door to and thinking that next time I'm here, it will be over. We will have said goodbye to Gran for good.

We take the lift down, when we would normally use the stairs. At the bottom, Graham – Maggie's boss – stands in the lobby, waiting for us. He nods at us as we go by and I smile at him. Mum puts her hand on his arm.

We walk, the three of us, along the familiar route to Godolphin Terrace and there we see the two black cars, pulled up outside Gran's house. The first holds her coffin and the second is empty, waiting for us. The smartly-dressed funeral director staff stand up straight when they see us, one of them opening the door to the back of the second car.

We file in but then – "Wait!" I say.

"Ada?" Mum asks.

"Just a minute." I jog to Gran's door, which I find locked as it never would have been when she was here. I scrabble in my bag for her key and I go in.

The house is empty. It still holds her furniture; her chair by the window, the old three-seater, and all her pictures and ornaments, and that reliable ticking clock, but it's empty. I won't find her here.

Nevertheless, I go around all of the rooms, finding myself saying thank you to them, for all of the moments of happiness I've had here, and for holding my mum and my uncle and my gran so safely after my grandad had died. I close each door softly and then I trot back down the stairs, closing the front door behind me but leaving it unlocked. "It doesn't really matter now, does it Gran?" I murmur.

The cars take a slow route around the town and as we follow the harbourside I realise people are stopping and standing; removing hats, bowing heads. As we pass them, some climb into waiting cars and follow on and by the time we are heading up and out of town and away to the crematorium, I realise we have formed quite a procession.

"We'll never fit them all in the crem," Uncle Laurie says.

"Standing room only," says Mum. "Not to worry, they can hear on the speakers outside."

I look behind. The number of people is making me nervous, but also proud. I know Gran has been a member of the community here for so many years, she's bound to be missed.

We draw up outside the crematorium and see Jude, Maggie, Stevie and Lucy waiting at the entrance. A respectable distance away there are at least twenty people, a few of whom I recognise, and their number swells as the people who have followed behind the funeral cars park up and come to join them.

The undertakers expertly move Gran's coffin onto the wheeled support, bringing it towards us. Maggie, Mum, Laurie, Jude, Stevie and I are the pall-bearers. Stevie had begged to be one and I managed to persuade Mum and Maggie that it would be OK.

"She's fourteen now," I said. "I know it's young but it's not as young as you're thinking. Remember what it was like being that age. If you can remember that far back," I'd said to Mum, hoping she'd take it in good humour and thankfully she did.

"Well OK then," she said. And she knows as well as I do that Gran would get a kick out of having an almost entirely female team of pall-bearers. Like a bride giving a speech at her own wedding, this is still often not the done thing, and I know that Gran would appreciate that.

"Besides," I pushed things a little further, "it's not exactly going to be heavy, is it? Gran was tiny."

"She was," says Maggie.

"Especially recently," Mum said sadly and I felt bad then, like I'd said something stupid. But I hope she understands that anything I say I mean in the best possible way because she knows just how much I loved – still love – my gran.

Now, the reality of the situation hits us all. I see Stevie looks scared and I realise she is shaking.

"Take a deep breath and just look ahead," I say. "Your

mum's in front of you and I'm behind you. It's all going to be fine."

I'm grateful for the chance to reassure her as in doing so I find my strength. I follow my own advice and take a long, deep breath, and then the music starts and it's time for action.

All fears of dropping the coffin or tripping up, or any of the other multitude of ways I've imagined this going wrong, are unfounded, and we are able to place Gran's coffin safely inside the crematorium.

As we file across to the front row of seats, the place fills up behind us. There are people standing around the edges and lining the back wall.

"Please be seated," smiles the celebrant, "if you can. And thank you everyone for coming. To those of you outside, I hope that the sun blesses us with an appearance soon, or at the very least that the rain doesn't decide to move in."

There is a good-natured chuckle at this.

"Now, it is my very great honour to be with you today, to celebrate the life of this clearly much-loved lady, Elise Morgan. Born in London, Elise has been a member of the community here in Cornwall for over eight decades and I think that we might be able to stop calling her an incomer by now." Another smile from the celebrant. More chuckling.

I hear a cough behind me and turn to see Gran's great friend Bill, handkerchief to his mouth, clearly trying not to cry. Maggie has turned too, and she briefly puts her hand on his.

The celebrant talks about Gran for a while and then she invites Uncle Laurie up to the front.

"My mum," he says, gesturing towards the coffin. "I'm sorry, I don't know why I did that. That isn't her, she isn't there. If she's anywhere, she's all around us. I like to think that, anyway. Now we've heard the facts about Mum's life. How old she was when she came across to Cornwall during the war; where she went to school, where she worked, got married, how many children she had… but what about Mum? Who was she? It's clear from the number of people here today that she was popular. We can definitely surmise that. But what made her so popular? Well she was kind, for a start. Incredibly kind, and thoughtful. She wasn't showy, and she wasn't judgemental. Mum had time and space for everyone. And this generosity came despite, or maybe even because of, her start in life. She never knew her dad, and her mum died during the war. When the war was over, she only had a place to go thanks to another kind woman, Angela Forbes, who took Mum in and eventually left her the house we were lucky enough to call home. So I suppose Mum did have some good fortune. She had a brief, and I'm sorry to say not very happy, marriage, and was widowed at an early age. And yet, despite all this, I honestly do not think I ever heard her complain. Do you, Louisa?" He looks at Mum, who is crying but manages to smile and shake her head. Uncle Laurie continues, "No, she was never one to complain. And she was also not one to accept limitations. Not from her gender, not from her age. It's only been recently that Lou and I have discovered Mum's love for night-time walks. Even in these last few years. And maybe these were her eventual downfall. She did, after all, fall ill on the beach one night, and she never recovered, but I think Mum would have thought it was worth it. She retained her independence really until the very end and I just can't say how proud I am of her. She was the most loving mother and she protected me and Louisa, through everything. Mum, you may have been short in stature, but you were the biggest, best and strongest woman alive. May your strength live on in all of us."

His voice had grown stronger and more sure as he spoke but now Uncle Laurie looks up and around the room, and he folds his piece of paper, and scurries back to his seat. He leans against Mum and lets her put his arm around him.

"Thank you, Laurie. That was beautiful," says the celebrant. She introduces the next piece of music and my heart is starting to really pound because I know what that means. It's my turn next.

As the notes fade away, I stand to walk to the front. Now that the moment is here, I feel less nervous, like the anticipation was the worst part.

"Hello everyone," I say into the microphone, looking out at a sea of faces. Every now and then I see somebody who I can think of as an anchor, to hold my gaze when I'm speaking if I start to drift away. Mum, Laurie, Maggie, Jude, Bill. Clara, and her boyfriend Joe. And then I see Josh, and Biba, who is openly weeping, and who is that with them? I'm amazed to see it's Josh's mum, Antonia. She smiles at me. I offer a weak smile in return. Then I think of the way she always calls me Ava, and the teddy which she left on my bed in lieu of the grown-up gifts she gave the others. I pull myself up. No granddaughter of Elise Morgan's is going to accept being belittled. I don't feel like using my notes now.

I look around, my chin up as I address the room.

"Thank you so much for coming today. We are blown away by how many of you are here to say goodbye to my beautiful grandmother, and I know she would be amazed to see how many lives she has touched. But although we are blown away, and although Gran would have been amazed, if I'm honest I am not surprised because as my uncle Laurie said, Gran was a wonderful person. And I may be biased but even objectively I know this to be true; I think we all do." There is much nodding around the room here. "And I am grateful every day for having her in my life. For being an inspiration, and a role model, and for letting me and my friend Clara come for holidays." I meet Clara's eyes here and we smile at each other. I've missed her. But I can't think about that now. "And for encouraging me with my artwork, and to follow my heart, and to be myself, and well... it's not really about me. But what I'm trying to say is what a huge influence she has had, and will continue to have, on me and my life. And I look around at all of you now and realise that it's not just me, and Mum, and Uncle Laurie, but it's so many people whose lives and hearts my gran touched. She believed in love, in friendship, in kindness and acceptance. It's so easy to talk about these things in these moments, but soon we'll be back at our jobs and our chores, and the little things in life will be bugging us once more, but if every now and then you're standing at the sink, or the ironing board, or answering a phone call to an annoying client, and you can remember Gran, and who she was and how she lived, I think that... I think that would be lovely."

I trail off here, having lost my thread a little and my

confidence having dropped suddenly away, like the sand shelves away on a beach.

There is another cough from Bill and I look at him, and he begins to clap. So too does the lady next to him, and then Mum and Jude, and Uncle Laurie, and everyone. Stevie is grinning and clapping so hard, and I can't quite believe it. As I walk back to my seat, I am smiling, but as I sit I feel my legs shaking like jelly.

"Well done," Mum squeezes my arm and then hugs me. "Well done," she says again.

As the celebrant begins to talk once more, I rewind the last few minutes, try to remember what I said. I feel my face going red but I remind myself again that this is not about me. Nobody is looking at me now, they're thinking about Gran. But I turn and I catch Josh's eye and he blows me a kiss and I think actually somebody is thinking about me. And I'm grateful.

We gather at the restaurant behind the beach for drinks to celebrate Gran's life, and Mum gives a toast there. She had not wanted to speak at the crematorium, which surprised me, but now I see she needed to save herself for this.

"You've all heard enough about my mum now, I'm sure," she says, looking at the large, framed photo of Gran which is sitting on the bar. "But please humour me for just a few moments while I tell you what she meant to me. We were close as can be when I was growing up. I was her little shadow. If I couldn't be with my mum then I wanted to be with her friend Maudie but I would always choose Mum above anyone. Then, as I became a dreaded teenager, I did all those things teens are meant to do, which for some reason my own daughter didn't–" Mum smiles at me briefly – "I rebelled. I started to pull away. And I went off into the world, got a degree, got a job, got another, and I lost my way a bit, and lost touch with what mattered. I would phone Mum, and I'd come back to visit, but for some reason I would choose to stay not with her but at a hotel. And I'd phone her, dutifully, but it would be those 'I can't stay on long' kind of calls, and she'd accept them with good grace. I could kick myself now, for those missed opportunities, but I know Mum would tell me off. She'd say there's no point, we can't go back, and she would be right. I'm so very happy that I've had a chance these last few years to try and put things right. We've spent time together and we've got to know each other again. And I finally realised truly what a woman she was. She made things happen. She was a trailblazer and if only I'd seen it earlier. I don't know what I believe, about where she might be now; if she can see us, look down on us, whatever. But I can picture her up there, shooting through the stars, blazing another trail that I can only look at in wonder. I am heartbroken that she has gone but she knew it was coming. That last day, in hospital, she said–" here my mum breaks off and I stifle a sob as I see her doing the same – "she said nobody can live forever. And she was right, of course. As always. But God, I wish we'd had just a bit more time. Now I just have to try and hold her here, in my heart and my mind, and hope that somehow, somewhere, I will see my mum again one day." Now everyone is in tears but Jude whispers something to my mum and she laughs. "I can't believe I forgot! This was meant to be a toast. To my mum. To Elise."

Mum raises her glass and the rest of us copy her, taking grateful gulps of champagne or orange juice, to wash down the lumps in our throats.

***

The nights are drawing in now, as Gran would say, darkness laying claim to more and more of each day. As it creeps closer this evening, I watch from the window, aware of conversations and laughter behind me but not wanting to join in yet not wanting to be alone either. Clouds drift across the bay as if they're looking for somewhere to rest for the night but, deciding this is not the place, they continue on their way, until the sky is clear and the stars are given the freedom to make their mark on it.

I feel a hand on my shoulder, and I turn.

"Alright?" Josh asks. "If that's not a stupid question."

"Yes, I'm OK thanks," I smile. "At least, I think so. It's weird, thinking I'll never see her again."

"I know. It seems impossible, doesn't it? When somebody dies who's been so much a part of your life, forever."

"At least nobody's told me she had a good innings." I smile.

"Urgh!"

"I know." I look down towards the beach, which is difficult to see now. That's where I found her, down on the sand below. I have been back there since; I've had to, for work, but I have tried very hard to compartmentalise things. Now, I have an idea.

"Want to come to the beach?" I ask my friend.

"Sure," he smiles.

"Just hang on." I pick up the nearest glass and I look for a spoon. Not finding one, I pull the clip from my hair, which unfurls itself over my shoulders. I tap the glass lightly, then – noticing it's had no effect – a little more firmly.

"Hi everyone," I say, not giving myself a chance to think this through. "I wanted to thank you all so much for coming today and for celebrating Gran's life. Now, as Uncle Laurie mentioned, Gran used to enjoy regular secret night-time walks on the beach."

This produces some smiles and some mutterings.

"She used to do this right up until she was in her nineties," I continue, "and I just think that says so much about what kind of person she was. So I'd like to invite any of you who would like to join me to come for a walk down there now, and remember Gran in a place which meant so much to her, doing something she loved."

"Hear, hear," says Bill. "Though I don't think my old legs are up to it."

"No pressure at all," I smile. "But anyone who would like to come is very welcome."

Around half the room – maybe more – begin to rally themselves. Glasses are uptipped into mouths and jackets and cardigans are retrieved and pulled on. I wait by the door and Mum and Uncle Laurie stand either side of me.

"Great idea, Ada," Uncle Laurie whispers.

We troop down the street, the three of us leading; Josh and Clara chatting behind me, I'm pleased to note. I could do with those two getting along. I think I'm going to need them.

Biba has stayed behind. The last time I saw her she was chatting to Bill, but I'm touched to see that Antonia has joined the group, and that she's walking with Jude.

I take Mum's arm and I think about how old she is; she and Uncle Laurie. I just hope they've inherited Gran's longevity, and not just that but her strength and drive.

We pick our way carefully down the steep slope and at the bottom I pull off my shoes, putting them neatly on the wall. Mum keeps hers on but Laurie takes his off and rolls up his trousers, sighing gratefully as his feet sink slightly into the soft sand. Lots of the others follow suit and soon the wall is adorned with a long line of shoes.

"Lead the way, Ada!" Josh calls, and I do, walking firmly towards the spot where I found Gran, though I don't feel the need to tell anyone that is where I'm going. I squeeze Mum's hand, and I think she knows why I've stopped. "Here," I say, stooping and selecting a stone. "For Gran." I pluck another for Laurie, and one for myself. It feels smooth and cool in my hand and somehow familiar. I curve my fingers tightly around it and walk on, down towards the waves. I press my feet firmly into the sand with each step, and I don't need to look to know that others are following. Those of us who wish to let the gentle fizzing water run across our toes, producing the occasional laugh, or shriek of delight.

Above us, the sky remains clear and a ghostlike gull sails across it, glowing in the light from the moon which sits high above the town, looking benevolently down like a proud mother.

Josh catches up with me and takes my hand. I smile and squeeze his fingers.

"Ow!" he complains.

"Don't be such a baby," I laugh.

"This is beautiful, a fully fitting tribute to a wonderful human being," he says.

That makes me well up.

"She was," I say. "And I know it sounds cheesy; a cliché, and incredibly unlikely, but I can't help but wonder if she is up there somehow." I gesture towards the sky.

"I'm quite certain she's out there," he says. "Energy can't just stop, can it? It must go somewhere."

"It was weird seeing her, when she'd died. Because she was clearly dead and yet my overwhelming feeling was that she was alright. I mean, that doesn't make any sense, does it?"

"Well, no, not if we're looking at things in a very straightforward kind of way. But who knows, maybe that was your inner voice connecting with something bigger than all that we know."

"I love the way you two think," Antonia's voice comes from behind us and I turn, surprised. She laughs. "I'm sorry to startle you, and to be eavesdropping. I really just wanted to come and see you Ada, as we haven't had the chance for a chat yet."

My god, she's actually called me by the right name. But what does she want to chat about? Josh peels away, saying he wanted to ask Jude about something.

"I know, I'm sorry, it's been a long and busy day," I apologise.

"Like a wedding," she says. "Sorry, that wasn't meant to be as tactless as it sounds. I just meant, it's one of those days when you don't have a moment to think or really talk to anyone. Which is why this was such a lovely idea, coming down here. And I really want you to know that I am so pleased that my son has you in his life and can talk to you the way he does."

"He's very important to me."

"I know, and he feels just the same about you. And that's what I wanted to talk to you about really."

Oh no, I think, remembering Biba's transparent attempt at matchmaking. Here it comes. My shoulders bristle at how inappropriate this is.

"It's just that, growing up, Josh felt like a bit of an outsider. He's not like his father or Andrew. I tried to connect with him; I'm a bit of an outsider myself you know. I'm not old money like them."

"Oh?"

"No, I've had to learn this way of life because, well because I love Jamie very much."

Is this how she's going to segue into it?

"I've tried to connect with Josh because he hasn't had it easy. I mean, I know he has everything he could wish for materially but it's that second son thing of course, and just… well, being Josh. He is a lovely boy, we both know that. And I've been so proud of how he's clung onto his ideals and always strived to be himself. Not easy, when there's a way of life carved out for you, and expectations. It seems like Biba understands this, bless her, and she and I both think it is wonderful that he has you. When he started at university and came back that first Christmas, you were all he could talk about."

"But…" I begin.

"No, no, don't worry. I understand. Honestly. I'm not trying to marry the pair of you off." We have reached the rocks near the end of the beach now and I realise that most of the others are some way behind us, scattered in

234

small groups chatting, or looking out to sea contemplatively. Antonia puts her hand on my arm. "I don't know if Josh has told you quite how difficult he found adolescence, and the struggles he had, being bullied at school..."

"No," I say lamely. I knew that Josh had not enjoyed school but he has never mentioned being bullied.

"He was an easy target. Not a natural sportsman. An arty type; a – vegetarian," she laughs but she looks sad. "He wanted to be pulled out of that school, and go to our local grammar instead, but my husband wouldn't hear of it. And Andrew, lovely Andrew, was years ahead of him at school and the type of boy who excelled at everything."

That doesn't surprise me.

"Anyway, I'm sorry, there must be lots of people here who you want to talk to, but I had to take this opportunity to thank you, for being the friend you are and for letting Josh be loved for who he is."

I'm touched. Really touched, and shocked. In fact, I don't know what to say.

"Just one more thing, Ada," she says carefully. "I am so sorry for mixing up your name so many times. It is unforgivably rude of me. But I had a friend called Ava when I was growing up. She meant as much to me as you do to Josh, but when I married Jamie, I let that friendship slide, and I shouldn't have. I really shouldn't have."

I think of what Gran said, about Maudie, and how important she was to her.

"It's why I gave you Bertrand," Antonia says.

"Bertrand?"

"Russell, the teddy bear. I mean to tell you about him but we were in such a rush that day. I wanted to give him to you, as he was a gift from Ava to me, when I got engaged, and I was meant to look after him and instead I put him in a box and all but forgot about him. It's what I did to my friendship with Ava, really. It's not good enough and I don't think I deserve him. I just had a feeling you'd take better care of him."

"That's lovely!" I say, and before I know it I'm hugging her. She returns the hug warmly, then takes my hands and steps back. "You look after Josh for me, OK? I don't mean you have to marry him! But will you make sure he's alright?"

"Well of course I will."

"Thank you my dear. Now I'd better get back to Biba or she'll have a few choice words for me!"

I watch Antonia walk across the sand, stopping briefly to speak to Josh and hug him before heading back towards the top of the beach.

"Well, that was a surprise, Gran," I murmur, turning my face up towards the stars, which twinkle back at me. And I go back towards the others: my family; my friends; Gran's friends. I feel buoyed by Antonia's words and revelations. All the while I thought she'd been looking down on me! It just goes to show that things are not always as they seem. But I had better try and remember where I've put Bertrand and make sure he has somewhere comfy to sit from now on.

As people leave the beach, retrieving shoes and trying unsuccessfully to brush the sand out from between their toes, I stay by the shore with Mum and Laurie, Jude and

Maggie, Stevie and Josh. We sit on the cold sand, not minding the damp. A long way out, I can see the lights of a ship passing by, and the lighthouse flashes intermittently above the rocks across the bay.

"Come on," Uncle Laurie says eventually. "It's getting cold. Let's go back to Mum's for a hot chocolate."

"Should we not go back and say our goodbyes to everyone?" Mum asks.

"It's fine," Jude says. "You've been perfect hosts all day. Now it's your time. Do whatever you want to do. If you like, I can go and tell them you're heading home."

"Would you?" Mum asks, ever the one to do things right. She kisses Jude and hugs her.

"Of course," Jude says into her shoulder. "Now go on, you lot, get going!"

"I'll come with you," Josh says. "I need to drive Mum and Granny back to the hotel."

And so it's just the five of us, and I think that here are all the people Gran loved most. We walk quietly up towards Godolphin Terrace.

"Are you alright?" I ask Stevie, thinking how young she is for all of this.

"I'm fine," she says, but I see her eyes are teary.

I take her hand. "Gran loved you, you know."

"I remember her helping me when I fell over and hurt my knee. When I was little."

"That sounds like Gran."

"She was really kind."

"She was."

Maggie turns and smiles at us. "You're both doing really well," she says. "Ada, that walk on the beach was perfect."

237

"Thank you," I smile.

We get to Gran's house and it's in darkness. That makes my stomach feel a little bit strange. And I feel bad for her, like she's missing out. She would have loved this; all of her favourite people coming to visit her.

"I know," Mum says, putting her arm around me. "I know."

"Right then, Ada," Uncle Laurie says, "I saw that you didn't lock the door when we were leaving."

"I, erm, sorry," I say sheepishly. "I didn't think you'd noticed!"

"I notice everything!" he grins. "I know Mum used to leave it unlocked but I wanted to lock it today; I'd planned to hand over these in a grand, ceremonial way, and ask you to unlock the door," he says, brandishing a small bunch of keys at me.

"Why?" I ask, laughing.

"Because this is yours now," he says.

I laugh again but notice that nobody else joins in.

"What?" I look at Mum and she nods.

"This house. Your gran's house. It's yours now. She left it for you."

2022

By the following Christmas, everything in Ada's life had changed again. Louisa was in a new relationship. With a woman.

Ada had met Jude a couple of times and she knew that she liked her, but it was still a bit of a surprise when Louisa told her what was happening. But Ada had grown up in a world where her friends knew it was fine to be whatever and whoever they were. No need to pretend to be somebody else in order to fit in. In fact, for some people at school it had almost been a badge of honour to be 'different' in some way. But Louisa wasn't one for labels and neither was Jude.

"I've just fallen for her," Louisa told her daughter, one rare evening when it was just the two of them. "For the person she is. My god, she annoyed me when we first met, and I know I annoyed her! An upstart from the City, used to getting my own way and being the boss!"

"This sounds like a storyline from a soap opera!" Ada had laughed.

"I know – it's a classic set-up. But honestly, I've never really looked at women that way, so it took me a bit by surprise as well. But she's... well, she's wonderful."

Ada had never heard her mum so gushy about anyone before. She thought back to the man her mum had been seeing in London, that night Ada had been with Ben, but thought it better not to mention him.

"Well, I'm happy for you Mum," she said, and hugged Louisa, but it meant even more that she had less of a place here. Her mum didn't need her as she once had, and in a way that gave Ada a freedom, to go and do as she pleased. Except she had no idea what that meant. She needed some sort of plan, with the end of uni being in sight, but that was as far as she'd got. Knowing that she needed a plan. It wasn't all that helpful.

"What does Gran think?"

"You know what? I don't think she minds a bit. She's happy for me, and she's happy to have me here. And, well, did you know about your great-gran? Mum's mum, Annabel? She and Angela Forbes, who left your gran her house, were... well... an item."

"What? I didn't think they had lesbians in those days!" They both laughed. "Maybe it runs in the family."

"I don't think it works like that," said Louisa, smiling and her cheeks reddening slightly.

"Mum, are you blushing?"

"No. Yes. Maybe."

"It suits you."

They'd seen in the new year together: Louisa, Ada, Jude and Elise, and it had been really nice. And seeing her mum happy with somebody set Ada to thinking that maybe she wouldn't mind meeting someone herself. She voiced this thought to Louisa one day.

They had gone out for a walk along the harbour and ended up walking to Tregynon, where they sat in the large window, looking out across the subdued gardens towards the grey, angry sea, and drank a Bloody Mary each to warm themselves up.

"Well, I never like to ask you. I mean, I assume there have been boys..."

"Not many."

"But you're quite a closed book you know, Ada."

"Am I?"

"Yes – to me, at least. And sometimes I blame myself, because I know you've been left to your own devices so much. But you're very self-sufficient, and that isn't a bad thing. You know you can always talk to me but as long as you're talking to somebody – Clara, Josh, whoever – then that's fine by me."

"Clara's a bit tied up with Joe these days."

"Ah well that happens too. I mean, I'm glad you're not looking at buying a flat with somebody at this young age but if she seems happy…"

"She does."

"Then we have to be happy for her. I know you must miss her, though. I never really had a friendship like yours, or like Mum had with Maudie."

"But now you've got Jude."

"Yes!" Her mum laughed, surprised. "I suppose I have."

"I mean, I know it's more than a friendship."

"But first and foremost, we are friends. And that's nice. So different to the men I've met."

"Even my dad?" Ada chanced.

"Well, that was really a non-starter."

"You know I don't need to know who he is, Mum, but I'd like to know how I got here! I don't mean the biology of it. But were you in a relationship, or did you really just pick up somebody and hope to get pregnant?" Ada was blushing now, feeling she was trespassing too far into her mum's privacy.

"I loved him, actually," Louisa said, looking her daughter in the eye. "But he was married."

"Oh."

"Yes. Oh."

"I wouldn't have thought you'd have done that; had an affair, I mean."

"No, well I didn't know that's what it was. I didn't know about his wife."

"Shit."

"Quite."

"And did you tell him about me?"

"I didn't get the chance," Louisa said. She took a deep breath. Jude was trying to rebuild her relationship with her daughter and maybe it was time that she became a bit more honest with Ada. "He died, you see. He was killed."

"No!" Ada was both horrified and intrigued. Though she tried not to give too much thought to her dad, the idea of him actually being dead was very strange. The thought of him being killed stranger still. "How?"

And so the whole story came out. How Gianni had flown back to New York and been caught up in the events of 9/11.

"You must have been devastated, Mum." Ada put her hand on Louisa's.

"I was. And I had no idea I was pregnant. When I found out, I thought my world was falling apart, but then it started to come back together in a different way. And you came along, and I wouldn't change that for the world." Louisa remembered how she and Elise had sat at this very table and had a heart to heart. There must be something about it. It was probably on a ley line or some such nonsense. She smiled slightly.

Ada smiled back, her eyes glistening with tears. "So was my dad American?"

"Yes."

A memory tugged at Ada. "Like that AJ guy."

Louisa looked shocked. "AJ?"

"Yes, wasn't that his name? The one you worked with."

"I'm surprised you remember about him!" Louisa tried to laugh lightly.

"Oh yeah, I forgot to tell you I met him."

"You...?"

"Yeah! Down here. On the beach. It was a couple of summers back and I don't know why he was on the beach in his work clothes but he came over... What's wrong, Mum?"

"What did he say to you?"

"Oh, I can't remember. Something about working with you. He was with a woman as well. They didn't stick around long." Ada wished she hadn't mentioned it; in truth she hadn't given him a second thought until now. It was very hard to read her mum's expression; was she angry? Ada wondered if AJ had played any part in Louisa's professional downfall.

Louisa downed the rest of her drink, wiping her mouth, which was a thin, tight line. "Come on," she said. "We'd better go."

"Alright." Ada drank as much as she could but it was strong and the ice made it too cold. She left her partially full glass on the table and followed Louisa outside.

"Mum," she said, desperate to recapture that closeness they'd been enjoying just minutes before. She slipped her arm through Louisa's and it slowed her down a little.

"Yes?" Louisa said. She turned to Ada with something like fear in her eyes.

"I'm sorry I asked, about my dad. It doesn't matter, Mum, who he was. I'm sorry that he let you down, and

I'm so sorry for him, that his life ended like that. But as far as me needing a dad, well it's never been important to me. You've always made sure I've got everything I need."

Louisa's eyes filled with tears. "Oh Ada," she said. "But there's so much that I haven't told you."

"It doesn't matter, Mum."

Ada pulled her mum close to her, so that Louisa's head rested on her shoulder, and it felt like a reversal of their relationship, the daughter becoming the comforter.

So her mum had been 'the other woman' too, Ada thought, just as she had been with Ben. But there was no way she would tell Louisa about that now. She was just glad she hadn't ended up pregnant as her mum had done.

Ada looked across the town, towards the cliffs where her mum and uncle and gran had once lived, in a house with a man they'd been so scared of. How strange, she considered, that her mum's dad had suffered a dramatic early death and now she'd found out that her own dad had too.

"It doesn't matter," she said again. "We all have our secrets, and I think that's OK."

Ada

"Come on in!" Josh says, "You're the guest of honour."

He is standing on the steps of a tall, stately-looking townhouse.

"I still can't believe this is yours!" I say.

"I know," he looks abashed. "Thanks to Granny."

"We both struck lucky with our grans."

"You can say that again."

"We both struck lucky with our grans."

"I can always revoke your invitation, you know. Now, come on, the crowds are gathering. Don't keep them waiting!"

Behind me are Mum and Jude, Uncle Laurie, Maggie, Tony, Lucy and Stevie.

"You're all very privileged to be invited to the opening night!" Josh reminds them, handing out glasses of prosecco – "I think my champagne days are behind me," he says.

"For now," I tell him. "You'll soon be raking it in."

The house I am walking into is Josh's home, and his means of earning a living. He's not yet decided in what direction he wants to go so he says he's going to try a bit of everything. He's applied for licences for running a catering business, and perhaps even small cookery classes, which he hopes will not be too hard as this used to be a bed & breakfast, so the kitchen is already fit for purpose. He's also keen to let some of the rooms on a long-term basis to 'arty types', and he's hoping that this month will be a kind of showcase for his beautiful house and will draw in the right kind of people.

The entrance hall is a work of art in its own right; a gorgeous wooden-framed stained-glass door leads the way into a cool, pristine, tiled hallway. To the right is the living room, which morphs into the dining room and leads into an open-plan kitchen with a partially glass roof which lets in a lot of light but is also subject to a lot of seagull poo.

Today, and for the whole of the month, Josh is opening his house three evenings a week, to showcase – well, I can hardly believe it, but to showcase my art.

All through the autumn and the winter and well into the spring, I've been working, up in Gran's attic, while Josh has been moving in here and sourcing furniture and decorating, and dropping round to mine for regular chats and discussions about the future. He's been there to see me on my knees, in tears, missing Gran and hating every single piece I've created. In fact, Josh has been extremely stern and has taken away pictures as and when I've finished them, framing them himself (another string to his bow as, amidst everything else, over the winter he's learned how to professionally frame pictures, taught by a lovely local man named Tobias, who if I didn't know better I'd say Josh has a bit of a crush on). He's stored the pictures here, up in his own attic, which he intends will be his living quarters once he's ready to let the other rooms out.

Now, finally, I'm happy(ish) with what I've created, while Josh says he's delighted and that everyone else will be, too. "I've invited the local rag, local radio, some influencers, all of them. You'll see, Ada, this is going to be the beginning of something beautiful."

"I hope so," I'd smiled, but I'm not holding out too much hope. "We'll see."

And we will see. Thanks to our grandmothers, both Josh and I have been freed up to wait and see... not that we are resting on our laurels but while many of our peers (not Sasha or Pippa of course) are taking on multiple jobs in a bid to pay their extortionate rents, we have the incredible luxury of fully paid-up places to live in. Which means that we just need to earn a living. Anything else is a bonus. It's a privileged position indeed.

"Come on," Josh says now, "I can't wait any longer."

He leads us into the lounge, and above the fireplace, in an ornate oval gold-leaf frame, is my portrait of Gran.

"Elise Morgan," reads a sign underneath. "1930-2024".

And underneath there is some information about Gran and how she came to be in Cornwall.

I look at Mum and see tears spilling from her eyes. "Oh Ada," she says. "She's beautiful."

"That's all Gran," I say shyly. "She was beautiful."

We stop, holding hands and reading what Josh has written about Gran, then we move on as I know that he is itching to show us everything he's done. Once I'd told him about my project and how it was inspired by the portraits in his own family home, it had got him thinking and really, this exhibition is the brainchild of us both.

The focus is Gran but the portraits are not all of her. They are of all the women who helped to shape her life, beginning with her mum, Annabel Morgan, and including people from her past who we have had to research a little, like her schoolfriend Violet and even Lady Whiteley, who gave her home over to become a school for girls when many people thought a girl's education need only be for a limited time, and a limited purpose. I painted Miss Hazlehurst, the headmistress whilst Gran was at school, and she looks down on us benignly as we make our way up the first lot of stairs.

On the first-floor landing, we find Angela Forbes — alone as the headmistress of the local school, and then again standing shoulder to shoulder with Annabel, their closeness implied but not explicit.

In the first bedroom up here are my portraits of Gran's best friend Maudie – as a young woman, and then as an older lady (as I remember her from my childhood) with her lovely husband Fred, and one of her with Gran. This one is based on a photo I have of them, from a year or so before Maudie died. Hopefully I have captured their youthful way of looking at life, and I have tried so hard to get that twinkle in Gran's eye.

As I look at that picture now, I feel like they are keeping a secret from the rest of the world. *It's all yours. Nobody's going to find out now.*

Josh has carefully hung the picture of Maggie and Stevie on the wall opposite Maudie, and has written some beautiful words about friendship and how age does not have to be a barrier.

"And now," Josh says proudly, as we traipse back onto the landing. With a flourish, he opens the front bedroom door. This is without a doubt my favourite room in the house. It has bay windows which look in one way back across the town and in the other direction down towards the sea. It made me draw my breath the first time I walked in and I do the same now as I see, alongside my portraits of Mum and Uncle Laurie (the honorary male in the exhibition), a row of three pictures which I have not created myself and which I have not been allowed to see until now. Pictures of me: a photo, a painting, and a pencil sketch.

"Do you mind waiting a minute?" Josh asks the others and he takes my hand and leads me towards the images. All three pictures are the same size and mounted in identical frames. The painting is by Josh himself, and it's of me reclining on a blanket.

"This is at your house!" I say, recognising the background of the horse and pony in the field.

"It is," he says. "It stuck in my head: an image of you just resting there on a summer's day, in a sort of liminal space, between student life and adult life, not knowing what was going to come your way."

"I still don't," I say. "It's beautiful though, Josh. Honestly, I love it."

"Really?"

"Really."

Next is the photo, which Uncle Laurie took. I turn and smile at him and he gives me a thumbs-up. I hate having my photo taken but he'd been very discreet with his camera on the day we scattered Gran's ashes: a beautiful day in the winter, when the wind was mercifully gentle and the sun was doing its best to provide us with some warmth. It looks like I'm listening to somebody, though they are out of shot, and my hair is loose around my face. My cheeks are pink and my skin looks clear.

"Did you use a filter on this?" I ask Laurie.

"No filter. It's just you."

I blush.

Finally, we look at the third picture which, secretly, I've been the most keen to see, even though I know I shouldn't be. This is by Archie and it's my head and shoulders, emerging from a body of water. My shoulders are bare, and my hair looks wet, slicked back from my face. Was he thinking of that moment at Josh's house, or the time in the sea? I'm glad I was already blushing, though I feel like my face must be growing redder by the moment, as I recall our day together. I haven't been in touch with Archie all that much but things are OK between us now. My feelings towards him thawed slightly on the day of Gran's funeral, when we had eventually returned to Mum's flat and found a bouquet resting against the door, with a card which read, 'I'm so sorry. From Alfie xx'.

"Josh. I can't believe you've done all this."

"Believe it!" he says, and he ushers everyone else in now. I show Mum and Laurie the portraits I've done of them, one each of them as teenagers and then as they are now – Mum with Jude, which makes her gulp – and one with them as children, Gran in between them, a strong, reassuring arm around them both.

I think again of where this idea began; of those dark, austere portraits in Josh's home, and the people behind them all. Their lives, their loves, their fears… all unseen.

Portraits, photos, social media; they can only show us so much about a person, and often only what they want us to see. Gran was somebody who would never have entertained the idea of joining social media, and she'd have laughed at the thought of a portrait of herself. She was a one-off; a loving, lively, modest woman with unseen depths of intelligence and determination. A friend to all, but never a pushover.

As I look at my painting of her now, as a young woman with her two children by her side, I think how difficult it must have been for her, in the post-war years, but I remember also what she said about my grandad, and how her marriage had shaped her view of relationships. She wasn't bitter but she was adamant that they are not everything. And I wonder how different things might have been if Davey Plummer had lived longer. If he hadn't slipped and fallen down that cliff. What would life have been like then, for my gran and my mum and my uncle? We will never know.

Elise

"Come on Elise!" Maudie is calling me, and smiling in that way she has; it takes me right back to those early days in Mr Fawcett's office, when she'd primed me to cover my chest and position myself just so, to prevent him peering down my top. Oh she was good fun, my friend.

"Hang on!" I say. "I'm not as nimble as I used to be."

And so she waits for me, at the door, while I pull on my shoes, groaning as I stand up and rolling my shoulders back, hearing the bones click into place.

It's dark out but I can hear the familiar voice of the sea, and I know exactly where we're going.

Maudie puts a hand on my arm. "Hang on," she says as a car rushes past, its headlights flashing across us. "Okay, let's go." We walk arm-in-arm to the pavement on the other side. She heads towards the steps.

"Hold on," I say. "I'm too old and creaky for that these days. Let's go the long way."

"Of course," she concedes kindly, and she looks me up and down. "You're showing your age, Elise!" she grins.

"I'm not ashamed of it."

"Nor should you be. Come on." She takes my arm and we take our time, the two of us. As we step gingerly down the slope, which is slightly slippery underfoot thanks to a thin layer of damp sand, I stop for a moment. Close my eyes. I can smell the sea and hear it too. What I wouldn't give for a swim. One more time, held in the loving arms of the waves.

"Shall we?" I ask Maudie, my eyes flicking open. I think her sense of fun has revived mine.

"We'll see." We begin to walk again and I realise it's not a good idea. Swimming at night never is, though I can't pretend I've never done it.

My eyes scan the sand which lies in darkness before us, and I look across to the cliffs, up to where I used to live, a long time ago. Then I look towards the sea, and the foaming tops of the waves which glow white in the darkness.

"Maudie!" I grasp my friend's arm, suddenly scared. "It's Davey." I am sure I've seen a figure, coming out of the water towards us.

"Hush," my friend says. "It's not. You're seeing things."

"Am I?"

"Yes," she smiles kindly. "He's long gone. He can't hurt you now."

"But we..."

"Hush," she says again. "Let it go."

We stand in silence for a while and I try to do as she says. I feel the soft breeze carried in by the waves, travelling across the beach and over my skin. I imagine it smoothing my wrinkles, of which there are many; soothing my worries, of which there are more. Easing my guilt, which I have never truly been able to leave behind.

I close my eyes again and I feel like I'm swaying. I want the elements to bend me to their will. I want to be a living part of this universe again, not somebody who watches from the window.

"Come on," Maudie says, "you're getting cold."

"I'm fine," I say, but my teeth are chattering.

"I shouldn't have brought you here," she says, anxious eyes on me.

"You should. You were right to. One last walk."

"But you haven't said goodbye," she says.

She's right. I need to see my girl – my girls. Louisa and Ada. And my beautiful boy. What was I thinking?

I open my eyes in a panic. "Maudie?"

"I'm still here," she says, "but I've got to go now. She's coming."

"Who? Don't go…" I reach for my friend but my hand remains empty.

"I'll see you soon, Elise. I promise. Hold on for now though, she's coming. She'll be here soon."

Shivering, I let myself collapse onto the soft, cold sand. I'm quite alone, I can see that now.

"You're not, Elise. You're never alone." It's Maudie again, but I'm too tired to open my eyes. I just need to remember what she said. Somebody's coming. I've got to hold on.

I'll do my best.

Acknowledgements

I have absolutely loved writing Ada's story. I love her, and Josh, and I even have a soft spot for Archie. I think most of us will have known an Archie at some point in our lives, whether or not we will have found ourselves in a similar situation to Ada is another matter...

I remember my own university days, and school days, so vividly, and it always amazes me how many vivid memories I have from that short time. Is it because work dulls our senses? Or because while we're in our teens and early twenties we are still changing so much and things feel more intense? Despite having moved a few times growing up, I still have some lifelong friends from those days and as friendship is a key theme of this book, as well as many of my others, I wanted to mention a few important people.

On my first day at university I was lucky enough to find my next-door-neighbour was a young woman called Frances Corcoran. I still remember meeting her for the first time and I don't think we ever looked back. This summer my daughter and I spent a weekend in London with Fran and her partner Rob, who totally spoiled us both. It feels like a real privilege to have that time with them, and for Laura to be getting to know Fran (almost) as well as I do.

Also at university as the weeks went on I kept being asked if I knew somebody called Chris Smith, who was also studying philosophy. This mysterious, exotically named individual remained a stranger until the second semester when we met and became friends, having a short romantic relationship that year – until he dumped me; a fact I think it is important to remember. But we remained friends and we have now been married for seventeen years so if people ask what use philosophy is, I can always say it's a good way to meet your spouse.

I also want to mention my Biscuit Chatter group – Laura, Lisa and Helena – who I met in the first year of secondary school and whose friendship is still so important to me today. They were outraged that in the first book Elise reveals she is not a fan of Bourbon biscuits and thus the Biscuit Chat was born, inspiring a short scene in Ada's story. I have Lisa to thank for the Mint Club line (why would you put toothpaste on a biscuits?)

A special mention to Gennie Tarleton, who I also met at secondary school and who, unbelievably, died ten years ago this month. She was one of the very first friends I made in Bristol, and was a beautiful, fun and very funny person. I am so pleased to be in touch with her mum Min, and incredibly touched that Min reads and seems to enjoy all my books. Gennie will never be forgotten.

Also from those days, though we didn't go to school together, is my friend Jen. This book is dedicated to her and her family. Jenny and I met in Bristol when we were fifteen and not long after I moved back after uni, we shared a flat, along with her now husband Neil.

When I was sixteen my family and I moved back up to Yorkshire, where I did my A-Levels (there was no Ben Noble for me by the way – he is a genuine figment of the imagination!) and I met, amongst others, my friend Kathryn, who quickly became an important person in my life.

I want to thank you all for helping shape those formative years, and helping create so many memories – some of which might be better forgotten... You are family to me and although we're scattered far and wide these days whenever I'm with you it feels like coming home.

A more recent friendship (though scarily this one is already more than ten years old) is with the wonderful Catherine Clarke. Cover designer, fellow dog-walker, paddle-boarder, swimmer, and general all-round brilliant person, thank you for your friendship as well as all the gorgeous covers you've created for me and fellow Heddon authors.

More thanks, to more friends, who I have come to know through my books as they are my crack team of beta readers! Not every one of them can read every book but I am endlessly grateful for their help, support and generosity in giving their time so freely. This time round thanks go to (in no particular order): Mandy Chowney-Andrews, Tracey Shaw, Jean Crowe, Amanda Tudor, fellow author Nelly Harper, Kate Jenkins, Ginnie Ebbrell, Rebecca Leech, Alison Lassey and Hilary Kerr.

I have a plan to one day host a beta readers' thank you party – I just need to sell a few more books first!

And lastly, as always, thanks to my dad, Ted Rogers, who once again has read through my final manuscript, to pick up on and help me correct any errors that have slipped through the net. Thank you Dad, for your help with this, your endless support of my writing, and for everything else as well.

This list of great people is not exhaustive – there are many other friends and family I have not mentioned here who I love dearly – so I have to conclude I'm a very lucky person. I am sure that all of you influence my writing and story-telling in many ways and there are little touches in every one of my books which should mean something to one or more of you.

Thanks and love to you all.

Coming Back to Cornwall

Books One to Ten

Available in print and on Kindle

The whole Coming Back to Cornwall series is being made into audiobooks so you that you can listen to the adventures of Alice, Julie and Sam while you drive, cook, clean, go to sleep… whatever, wherever! Books One to Five are available now.

Connections
Books One to Three

Each story focuses on a different character all inextricably linked within the small Cornish town they call home.

What Comes Next

An introduction to the Hebden family as they celebrate their first Christmas without much loved wife and mother, Ruth. Set entirely on Christmas Day, at the long barrow where Ruth's ashes have been placed. It is Ruth herself who tells the story, seeing and hearing all.

This short, festive story is an exploration of another side of this time of year normally packed with family, friends and festivities. It is nevertheless uplifting and engaging, and full of Christmas spirit.

The first full-length novel begins with an illicit kiss, with Ruth its only witness but unable to say or do anything about it. As her family begin to find their way through their grief and navigate new situations and changing relationships, Ruth herself has much to learn as she comes to terms with her new situation and the fact that she can now only watch as life moves on without her.

Individual novels

Writing the Town Read: Katharine's first novel. "I seriously couldn't put it down and would recommend it to anyone who doesn't like chick lit, but wants a great story."

Looking Past - a story of motherhood and growing up without a mother. "Despite the tough topic the book is full of love, friendships and humour. Katharine Smith cleverly balances emotional storylines with strong characters and witty dialogue, making this a surprisingly happy book to read."

Amongst Friends - a back-to-front tale of friendship and family, set in Bristol. "An interesting, well written book, set in Bristol which is lovingly described, and with excellent characterisation. Very enjoyable."

Printed in Great Britain
by Amazon